Seasons of Magic

Mother Nature's Magic

"Good morning, Erin. Another good picking, I see."

"Yes, it is," Erin said, setting down two cereal bowls, each filled to the brim with berries. "I keep expecting the berries to run out, but every day there are more, almost as though they're magic bushes."

Evangeline's eyes twinkled as she replied, "They are magic, Erin. Natural earth magic, that is," she said, laughing from deep down in her belly. Erin was always amazed at that laugh which was so big yet came from a woman who was so small.

"What do you mean, earth magic?" Erin asked, settling down into a chair, eager for one of Evangeline's lessons . . .

About the Author

Laurel Ann Reinhardt has been interested in alternative spirituality since her childhood. A goddess-mother twice over, this book grew out of experiences with her oldest goddess-daughter, and her participation in a women's cross-quarter day celebration group (of which she is a founding member).

She has a Ph.D. in psychology and is a practicing psychologist and writer. In her work as a psychologist, she uses dreamwork and ritual to help people listen deeply to themselves in order to reconnect with their soul dreams, those yearnings that give meaning and purpose to life. She also writes about the changing face of psychology and its relevance for today's world. Her essays, articles, and columns have been appeared in *Twin Cities Wellness* and *Northern Sun* newspapers, *The Edge*, *The Phoenix*, and *Today's Health and Wellness*. She is a contributing author of the forthcoming book: *Thundering Years: Rituals and Sacred Wisdom for the Journey into Adulthood*.

To Write to the Author

If you wish to contact the author or would like more information about this book, please write to the author in care of Llewellyn Worldwide and we will forward your request. Both the author and publisher appreciate hearing from you and learning of your enjoyment of this book and how it has helped you. Llewellyn Worldwide cannot guarantee that every letter written to the author can be answered, but all will be forwarded. Please write to:

Laurel Ann Reinhardt
℅ Llewellyn Worldwide
P.O. Box 64383, Dept. 1-56718-564-9
St. Paul, MN 55164-0383, U.S.A.

Please enclose a self-addressed stamped envelope for reply, or $1.00 to cover costs. If outside U.S.A., enclose international postal reply coupon.

Many of Llewellyn's authors have websites with additional information and resources. For more information, please visit our website at www.llewellyn.com.

Seasons of Magic

A Girl's Journey

Laurel Ann Reinhardt

2001
Llewellyn Publications
St. Paul, Minnesota 55164-0383, U.S.A.

FIRST EDITION
First Printing, 2001

Book design and editing by Connie Hill
Cover design by Kevin Brown
Cover and interior art by Jan Stamm

Library of Congress Cataloging-in-Publication Data
Reinhardt, Laurel Ann, 1950–
    Seasons of magic: a girl's journey / Laurel Ann Reinhardt. — 1st ed.
        p.   cm. —
    Summary: Twelve-year-old Erin spends a year working with an old wise woman to learn about her family's Wiccan religion.
    ISBN 1–56718–564-9
    [1. Witchcraft—Fiction.] I. Title.
PZ7.R2765 Se   2001
[Fic]—dc21   2001016491

Llewellyn Publications
A Division of Llewellyn Worldwide, Ltd.
P.O. Box 64383, Dept. 1-56718-564-9
St. Paul, MN 55164-0383, U.S.A.
www.llewellyn.com

♲ Printed in the United States of America

Dedication

To Erin, my goddaughter, who, through her own spiritual journey, inspired this story;

to my own Evangeline, who said, "The more beautiful the story, the truer it is";

and to the members of my Wishcraft group: Anne, Cari, Charlie, Jim, Kate, Mary Ellen, Mike, Tim, and Tom, who supported me during the writing of this book.

Contents

Why?

I don't know why I let my mother talk me into this, Erin thought nervously as she crossed the wide, wrap-around porch at the front of Evangeline's house. Erin reached out a gloved hand for the door knocker, then pulled back quickly when she realized it was a figure of a snake curled back on itself, swallowing its tail. She hesitated briefly, glancing around to see if anyone was watching. *I could still leave,* she thought. *Coward!* came the immediate reply. *If you want to know, you have to do this.* She took a deep breath and, with a trembling hand, reached out again, letting the brass snake fall as she stepped back.

Part of her was excited to see what other oddities lay behind the unusual door, while another part of her just wanted to turn around and run before the door opened, exposing her to whatever was behind it.

Why can't I be like my friend Rachel? Erin thought. *Why can't I just believe what she believes? Why do I have to know what lies behind wooden doors with snake door knockers? Why, why, why?*

Erin's tension reached such a state that when Evangeline finally opened the door, it was like opening a vacuum. Erin found herself propelled into the old woman's living room. She whirled around to face Evangeline, blurting out her need before she could chicken out.

"I just had to talk to someone, Evangeline, and Mom thought it would be best if I talked to you. I'm so upset and confused, I don't know where to start. You just have to help me, I . . ."

Erin stopped suddenly, aghast. Here she was telling an eighty-year-old woman, a woman of acknowledged wisdom in spiritual matters, what she had to do. Suddenly, all of the fear and hesitation Erin had experienced at Evangeline's front door came back in a rush. She was about to apologize when she noticed that Evangeline was smiling. Erin relaxed enough then to realize that she was actually taller than Evangeline, who had always seemed so huge. And the wisps of gray hair that had escaped from their clasp reminded Erin of her grandmother.

"We'll start with some tea," was Evangeline's response. "Then, when you've caught your breath, you can tell me all about it. Come on in the kitchen while I get things ready."

In the sunny, warm kitchen, Erin felt soothed as she watched Evangeline in the familiar task of tea-making. Soon she had her chilled hands around a steaming mug and was telling Evangeline her troubles.

"We shared in school today about what we did over winter vacation. Rachel talked about Christmas and Jesus, and how it's His birthday, and how special that is because He's God's son. She says He is God's gift to the world, and that's why she and her family exchange gifts, as a reminder of that. And I can see why that makes Christmas so special to her."

Evangeline nodded.

"Then it was my turn. I had been real excited to tell about our celebration of Winter Solstice with the tree and candles, and the gift blanket and all, but once I was talking, I realized that I didn't know why we celebrate solstice. There must be a reason for it all, some point to it, but I don't know what that is."

"You mean, there must be a better reason than 'we've done it before and it's fun.' Some reason bigger than all of us."

Erin nodded, appreciating Evangeline's quick understanding. "What made it even worse was that on the way home, Rachel and I ran into Jonathan. He's an older boy who was held back a year so he's in our class. Anyway, he made fun of me and our solstice celebration all the way home, saying our house would burn down from the candles on the tree, and that my parents should have given me away on the gift blanket. I was really glad Rachel was there. She just kept telling me to ignore him, that he didn't know what he was talking about. But I could tell that she didn't understand about our solstice, either."

"I can see why all that would be so upsetting, since you are already having doubts on your own," said Evangeline. "Now, tell me how I can be of help."

"Well," Erin started slowly, gathering her thoughts, "Mom and I thought you might be the best person to teach me about our celebrations."

"Why can't she or your godmother, Sarah, help you? They both know about these things, too."

"Oh, they do, for sure, but Mom thought you might be more objective than either of them."

"You mean I might be more inclined to let you find your own way, rather than insisting you understand things as I do," Evangeline said thoughtfully.

"Right! Besides, you're a lot older and wiser than Mom and Sarah. You're the one who taught them all they know." After a moment Erin blushed, wondering if she might have offended Evangeline by saying she was so much older.

As if she could read Erin's mind, Evangeline responded, "Oh, don't worry about offending me, child. After all, I am a lot older. Why, I must be twice their age. Now, on to your request. You already know that I celebrate the eight seasonal earth festivals, just like your mother and Sarah. Imbolc is coming up next, so I guess that's where we'd begin. . . ." Evangeline paused.

"Great! So what is Imbolc, what do I do?" Erin asked in a rush, trying to look excited and enthusiastic, while inside she felt as though something was chewing its way through her stomach.

"Wait a minute, slow down," Evangeline said solemnly. "I haven't agreed to do it yet."

Sheepish, Erin blinked into the old woman's steady eyes. "And, you may not want me to help after you hear what my ground rules are."

Erin suddenly felt wary. "Ground rules?" she asked, incredulously.

"Yes, ground rules. You seem to be pretty serious about this. Well, so am I. So, there will be ground rules."

"Like what?"

"Well, you know it takes a full year to celebrate all of our festivals, so the first ground rule is that we both agree to work together for one full year. That means that the final celebration in our year of work will be Winter Solstice of next year. Do you think you can agree to that?" asked Evangeline.

Erin nodded silently, feeling very grown up all of a sudden.

"Good. Now, in return for the guidance I give you, you will need to give something as well. I don't know yet what that will be, and there may be more than one, but such sacrifices tend to fit in with what you will be learning."

Before Erin could speak, Evangeline continued. "Now I don't want you to give me your answer to this ground rule right away. This is not an easy decision to make, so I want you to sleep on it. Tomorrow will be soon enough to tell me what you decide."

With that, Erin found herself being whisked through the house, into her coat, and out the front door, which banged shut behind her.

I guess I don't get to ask any more questions, thought Erin, as she went down the steps. *I just have to decide. But how do I decide without much information? I wonder what kind of sacrifices she's talking about anyway? Surely they can't be too hard, since I'm only twelve. Still, it's tough to make a decision without knowing more. Maybe I could ask Sarah to help me. . . .*

Erin stood at the end of Evangeline's sidewalk, wondering what to do. In the end, she turned toward home, knowing she had to make this decision on her own.

That night, Erin lay awake in her room for a long time. By bedtime she knew she had already made her decision when she knocked on Evangeline's door; she intended to spend the year learning from the old woman. What kept Erin awake were all of the unknowns: *What sacrifices would she have to make? What would she learn? Would she be able to meet all of the challenges that lay ahead? Would she come away with a stronger sense of who she was and how she fit into the world? Would she eventually know her god in the way Rachel knew hers?* She finally fell into a fitful and dream-charged sleep.

Breathwork

Two weeks later, in mid-January, Erin found herself sitting in Evangeline's kitchen once again, this time with a mugful of hot chocolate in her hands. She sneezed while reporting to Evangeline on what she had been doing to prepare for Imbolc.

"I know you said to be still at least ten minutes a day, especially around sunset, so I will notice how the days are getting longer and how the light is changing and how I am changing in response, but it's really hard. There is so much going on now. For some reason we are getting more homework since winter break, and because it is staying light later, Rachel and some of my other friends want to play outside right after school until they have to go home for dinner. This week we went ice skating twice, sledding once, and had a snowball fight. I even hit Jonathan without getting hit myself," Erin ended proudly.

"That does sound like fun," Evangeline said thoughtfully.

"Well, not all fun, I guess. At least, it wasn't so much fun at the time. See, Rachel and I were skating on the lake near school. There was nobody else there, so we were practicing spins. We're not very good at them yet, so we don't want anybody watching us, especially Jonathan. So of course he showed up. We stopped our spins and just tried to ignore him, but he kept coming closer and closer, and even brushed me once. He didn't knock me down, or anything, but his being there at all kind of ruined our fun. So, we left, and he followed, yelling things at us, like how we were never going to make the Olympics. Rachel finally got so upset that she made a snowball and threw it at him. Boy, was I surprised. She usually doesn't do things like that. Anyway, Jonathan started throwing snowballs at us, then, so it became self-defense. I kept running and dodging and picking up snow as I went, and got off a good one just before I turned the corner for home. I just quit and ran home. I didn't think my mother would approve."

"That's quite a story," was all Evangeline said.

When Evangeline didn't say any more, Erin went on. "And then I got this cold. I really have trouble concentrating when I'm sneezing and blowing my nose all the time." As if to prove her point, Erin pulled out a handkerchief and wiped at her nose. "I can't even write the poem we were assigned for English this week, and it's due tomorrow."

At this, Evangeline sat up, her eyes widening. "A poem, you say! What a perfect assignment. I wonder if your teacher celebrates Imbolc."

For the first time that day, Erin's curiosity got the better of her. "What do you mean, it's a perfect assignment?"

"Well, remember what I said about Imbolc being a time of inspiration. Literally, that means drawing in breath, which is life, which is creativity. ... ."

"Which is what you need to be able to write a poem," Erin finished, her eyes sparkling with excitement.

"Exactly. And what do you need to be inspired?" asked Evangeline.

"You need to sit still and listen," Erin said meekly, "just what I haven't been doing."

"And just what winter is so perfect for," added Evangeline.

Erin brightened a little. "So maybe that's what my sacrifice is for this time of year. I need to be quiet and listen instead of rushing around with my friends so much. To tell the truth, it is wearing me out a little. Is there anything you can teach me to help me with this?"

"Of course there is! And really, the sacrifice doesn't have to be very big. Like I told you before, ten minutes a day is plenty. Now, why don't we go in the other room and I'll teach you a brief meditation."

The "other room" was one Erin hadn't seen before. It was a little sunroom off the kitchen that, on a sunny day, would be bathed in warmth just like the kitchen had been that first day. Today, however, it lay in shadows and had a slightly mysterious feeling. In one corner sat a small table covered with a multicolored scarf on which were some candles, a crystal, and an incense burner. *Evangeline's altar*, thought Erin briefly, before taking in the rest of the room. On either side of the table were two incredibly comfortable-looking chairs, wooden rockers with thick, sea-green, cotton-covered cushions on both bottom and back. The only wall that wasn't taken up with either a door or windows was totally given over to bookcases so full that the books had overlowed into a stack on the floor at one end. A single lamp hung from the ceiling over the small table.

"This is my favorite room," Evangeline said. Erin felt the same way even though she hadn't seen the upstairs of Evangeline's house.

"Have a seat," Evangeline said. Erin took the chair nearest the door, and found herself staring out the side window at a mammoth old oak tree. Once again, she sneezed.

Evangeline settled herself in the other chair and began to rock, very slowly. Erin soon found herself rocking in unison with the old woman. After a while she became aware that her breathing had slowed to match the rocking of the chair. It was slow, rhythmic, and even, flowing in as she rocked back, and out as she rocked forward. In what seemed like only a few moments later, she noticed that Evangeline had stopped rocking.

"Aren't you going to teach me?" Erin asked.

"I just did," Evangeline replied.

Erin was about to argue when she noticed that she could barely see Evangeline. It was almost dark. When they started it had only been 4:30. "What happened?"

"We rocked and breathed."

"That's all?"

"What more would you like?"

"Some inspiration; I still have a poem to write for tomorrow."

"You breathed; the rest is up to you," Evangeline said. "That's enough for today."

"Well, I do feel better," Erin said, sniffing to test how her nose was doing. "And I sure did notice the change in light today. It is getting dark later, isn't it?"

Evangeline nodded, as she ushered Erin out of the room. "Come and read me that poem, when you get a chance."

Erin turned and smiled as she put on her jacket. "I have to write it, first. But . . . maybe," she said, hugging the old woman. "I'll see you soon," she said as she ran out the door, in a rush to get home and get down to work.

Three nights later, on February 2, Erin sat on the floor in front of Evangeline's fireplace. A small fire was burning; along with an array of candles, it provided the only light in the room. Evangeline had been tending the fire with words, the last of which Erin now caught.

". . . as the sun lights the day, and as a similar light shines within each of us. Thank you for your generous gifts."

Evangeline turned to Erin. "Do you have a gift to offer?"

Erin nodded and pulled a piece of paper out of her pocket. Solemnly she opened the paper, smoothed it out, and began reading.

The Light

Always here, whether distant or near
Breathe it in, let it touch winter
And watch the heart rise
To greet summer's dawn.

The silence stretched out so taut that Erin thought she would break. "It isn't very long," she began apologizing, when Evangeline silenced her with a wave of her hand.

"It is a gift, and a truly inspired one, from the light to you and back again. It is more than enough."

Erin felt great joy sweep through her. She didn't need to apologize. It was enough. Basking in that knowledge, Erin had to force herself to pay attention to the next thing Evangeline said.

"Just a little more teaching, Erin. Imbolc is the time of year for initiation, the beginning of taking part in sacred ceremonies. It seems very appropriate that we are starting our year's journey together at this time. It feels to me like that poem was your

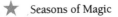

gift of initiation, an indication that you are accepted and on the right path. But there are many levels of participation, with just as many levels of initiation. It seems to me that part of this year's task for you will be to decide at what level you want to participate; whether or not you want to continue after this year and go deeper."

Erin nodded solemnly and turned her gaze back to the fire. The flames reminded her of the joy she had felt just a few minutes ago. Already that seemed long ago as she wondered what the remaining seven festivals would bring.

Welcoming Life

Late February found Erin and Evangeline walking through the local bird sanctuary together. They both agreed it was one of their favorite places, so it seemed a natural place to go to talk about Spring Equinox, the next earth festival in their cycle of celebrations.

"The only thing I know about Spring Equinox is that you can stand eggs on their fat ends," said Erin. "Mom and I have a contest to see who can balance the most before we run out of eggs. At first it seems impossible, but once you get a feel for it, you just know when the egg will stay up. It's so funny to come into the kitchen and see five or six eggs standing upright. Then a day or two later you find them all fallen over again."

Evangeline smiled. "I love doing that too, Erin, because that's what the equinoxes are both about, balance. Spring and fall are the two times of year when sunlight and darkness are equally balanced, so we are poised between life and death. In the spring, we are balancing on the verge of life. See here," Evangeline said, grasping the branch of a tree in her hand, "the snow isn't even gone, but this tree is preparing for life."

Erin took the branch from Evangeline and peered closely. "What am I looking at?" she asked.

"The buds—the places where the leaves will come out. If you had looked at them a week ago, you'd see the difference now. They are swelling, and soon they will burst open with the first green of spring."

Erin looked again, then moved on to a nearby bush. "Oh, I can see it here. The buds on this bush are definitely bigger than the buds on the trees. I'll start paying attention and check them each time I walk through here."

"Good, that's one way to prepare for spring. What else can you do?"

"Well," Erin spoke slowly, giving thought to her words, "this is a bird sanctuary. I guess I could do something to welcome the birds on their way back from the south." Erin looked around. "Actually, it's kind of messy in here, with all those bottles and cans and cigarette butts and whatnot. I sure wouldn't want to stop here if I were a bird. So, each time I come through I could pick up some litter and throw it out."

"That's an excellent idea, Erin."

The next day, after school, Erin headed for the bird sanctuary with a plastic bag in her pocket. She was only half a block from the sanctuary when she saw a blonde-haired boy walking toward her on the sidewalk. *Jonathan,* Erin thought with despair. Although she usually made every attempt to avoid him, to do so today would mean not going through the bird sanctuary as she had promised herself she would do. She took a deep breath and picked up her pace, intending to just march right past him.

"Wait a minute, Erin," said Jonathan, stepping in front of her. She slowed down slightly, moving to her left, still hoping to get by. When Jonathan moved with her, she tried stepping to her right, slowing still more. Once again, he blocked her path. Erin stopped, realizing there was no way out. She was going to have to talk to him.

"Where are you going in such a hurry?" Jonathan demanded.

"If you must know, I'm on my way to the bird sanctuary," replied Erin, chin up and looking right in Jonathan's blue eyes as Evangeline had suggested she do.

"The bird sanctuary, huh? Me and my friends go there all the time."

Erin took a step back, wrinkled her nose, and looked at Jonathan quizzically. "You like the bird sanctuary?"

"Oh, yeah, it's a great place to hang out."

Erin nodded, her initial surprise ebbing away. "I suppose you and your friends are the ones who leave bottles and cans in there."

"If they're empty, yeah, why not?"

Erin suspected he was probably baiting her. After all, he had heard all the lectures in school on littering and recycling just like she had. Still, she couldn't help responding to the taunt. "Because other people go in there, too, and it's ugly. Besides, the sanctuary is really for the birds, not us."

"You bet it's for the birds. It's a real drag in there unless you're partying."

Erin had had enough. She stuck her hands in her pockets, gritted her teeth, put her head down, and once again tried to get past Jonathan. He grabbed her left arm to spin her around. The hand came out of the pocket, along with the plastic bag. Erin groaned and grabbed at it, but Jonathan was quicker.

"What's this," he cried gleefully. "Don't tell me, let me guess. You're going into the bird sanctuary to pick up litter. That's really nice of you to clean up after me."

Erin held her tongue. She made a quick grab, took hold of the bag and ran, hearing Jonathan's jibes fading behind her. When she reached the entrance of the bird sanctuary she was out of breath and shaking with anger and frustration. Taking some deep breaths to calm herself, Erin entered the sanctuary through the tall, turnstile gate. She began to make her way through the sanctuary, picking up a gum wrapper here, a bottle or can there. Her progress was slow and lethargic.

I'm not picking up after that pig, Erin had to remind herself. *I'm doing this for the birds and for the earth, not for him.* Still, when she came to a large collection of pop cans, she found herself feeling resentful. *Why can't he and his friends do this for themselves,* she wondered, smashing one of the cans under her boot. *They carry them in okay, what's so hard about carrying them out?* She sighed, realizing once again that it didn't matter. *Maybe this is my sacrifice this time,* she thought, *picking up after someone I really don't like.* With that, Erin strengthened her resolve, and started back to her task with a renewed sense of joy. *After all,* she thought, *I'm doing this for me, too, 'cuz I like walking through here better when it's clean.*

A little over a week later, Erin walked home from school with Rachel. "I've missed walking home with you, Erin. It seems like the only time I've gotten to see you in the past week is at school. I know you've been real busy with Evangeline and preparing for the equinox. How is it going?"

"It's actually fun, and a lot easier than preparing for Imbolc. I'm doing something I really enjoy and care about."

"You mean picking up the litter in the bird sanctuary?"

"Yeah. I really like it in there, and it feels like I'm helping to make it a nicer place for the birds and all of us."

Rachel was quiet for a while. "I think that's really a great idea, Erin. I know I like it better in there when it's clean. I wonder . . . did you tell Jonathan what you were doing?"

Erin grimaced and barked out a laugh. "Well, I wouldn't exactly put it that way. He caught me on my way into the sanctuary one day and kind of forced it out of me. Then he had the nerve to thank me for picking up after him and his friends, because they go there. I couldn't wait to get away from him."

Rachel paused again, looking thoughtful. "Erin, you're not going to believe this, but I saw him going into the sanctuary on Sunday with a garbage bag in his hand. It was almost like he was sneaking in. He looked around, like he wanted to make sure nobody was watching, and then he hurried in and ran out of sight."

"He didn't see you?" Erin asked.

"No. I was hiding behind a tree because I didn't want him to see me, you know?"

Erin nodded; she knew exactly.

"I wanted to go into the sanctuary myself, but after he went in I hung back for a while, waiting to see if he would come out. Sure enough, about five minutes later he came out, and it looked like he had something in the bag. I figured it was some unlucky animal, but I didn't have the nerve to go up to him and ask. He left pretty fast and I forgot about him. I was just glad to be able to go for my walk. Now I wonder. Do you think he was picking up litter?"

Erin thought a moment, then nodded. "It's hard to believe, but I think that's exactly what he did. I went in there yesterday on my way home from school, and there were only a few scraps of paper blowing about, no bottles or cans." Erin paused again. "I bet he and his friends were there Saturday night, and he went back on Sunday to pick up after them."

"Yeah, I bet you're right. He still wanted to be one of the guys, so he couldn't pick up the litter that night. And that's why he was looking around so hard on Sunday. He didn't want to get caught by any of his friends. Well, what do you know," Rachel said with a little smile.

"Hard to believe, all right. I bet he wouldn't want us to know, either. After all, he has this image to protect with us, too. But he might not be as bad as we think, huh?" Erin said, shaking her head.

"Maybe not," said Rachel, "but I still hope we don't run into him on the way home."

The morning of March 21 found Erin once again in the bird sanctuary with Evangeline. It was a little before dawn.

"Well, Erin, I must say, you've done a nice job in here," Evangeline said, turning all the way around.

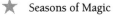

"Thanks. It does look nice, doesn't it? And I keep watching the buds on the trees and bushes. There's been quite a change in just the few weeks I've been paying attention. I've even found a few leaves starting to open up."

"Well, then, we really are balanced on the edge between death and life, aren't we?"

Erin nodded, looking briefly in the direction of sunrise. "Just like we're on the edge between dark and light right now." Evangeline smiled. "I noticed something else in these past few weeks." Evangeline waited. "I used to think of people as good or bad, like I was good and Jonathan was bad. But I think good and bad are more balanced than that. I mean . . . " Evangeline still waited. "I mean, that each of us has some of both."

"How did you decide that?" Evangeline asked.

"Well, you remember Jonathan?" Evangeline nodded. "I used to think he was all bad, just plain mean and nasty. Then Rachel told me something that makes me think that he's been coming into the bird sanctuary and cleaning up, too." Erin took a deep breath. "The other piece is harder to talk about, because it's about me. I used to think I was this really nice person. But after I found that out about Jonathan, I realized that I haven't been particularly nice to him. Not that it would be easy

27

to be nice to someone who acts like he does, but I go out of my way to be mean, and I call him names behind his back. So, I've decided to try and be different with him."

Just then, the top of the sun became visible above the horizon. "That's a wonderful resolution for equinox, Erin. Not an easy lesson, but you learned it well."

As they stood together, arms around each other's waists, watching the sun rise, Erin wondered, *Just how am I going to be different with him? What do I want? Do I want us to be friends?* Erin shuddered slightly, and held on tighter to Evangeline, who also seemed to be trembling. *Must be the excitement,* thought Erin, as she leaned her head on Evangeline's soft shoulder.

Dance of the Heart

"So, what's next?" Erin asked, eyes sparkling and intent as she and Evangeline took a tour of the old woman's back yard.

"Next is Beltane, or Mayday, and it's about this," Evangeline replied, gesturing to her garden.

"Flowers?" Erin asked, surveying the crazy quilt of tulips, jonquils, asters, and many other flowers whose names she didn't know. There was also evidence of much more to come; shoots were pushing up through the soil everywhere.

"Yes, flowers. Tell me, what does it take for flowers to grow? What brings them back out of the earth to show themselves after the cold darkness of winter?"

Erin stopped walking and gave this some thought. "Well, I guess it's the rain and light and warmth . . ." Erin paused, turning to look at Evangeline for her reaction. As was so often the case,

Erin was unable to read anything in the beautifully etched face. But Evangeline's silence let Erin know that more was expected from her. After a little more thought, she added excitedly, "It's the change in the sun!"

Evangeline smiled broadly. "That's right, Erin. It's the change in the sun, which means more light, more warmth, more heat, all of which bring things to life. More than that, it's the way things are brought to life that is Beltane. During the summer, things grow steadily but slowly, leisurely, eventually reaching their fullness like a refined Southern lady."

"Like you."

Evangeline acknowledged the compliment with a smile, then went on. "In the spring, the growth is riotous, as if nothing can wait one more second to be out in the light. It's like one huge passionate celebration that spends itself quickly, and then makes way for what is to come next."

"Like the Mayday celebration we go to, with its parade and ceremony and activities. I've always enjoyed it, but never really knew what it was about." Erin paused, then added, "Now I think I'll enjoy it even more. That is, if I'll be able to go. What do you have planned for me, for us?"

Evangeline sat down on an old two-seater wooden swing, arranging her strikingly orange skirt about her. She motioned for Erin to join her. "Well, I actually thought the Mayday celebration would be perfect for what you have to learn this time. And that kind of settles the preparation, too."

"Of course," Erin burst out, "I can go to one of the workshops." She halted abruptly. "But that means I'd be expected to participate in the celebration in some way. I wouldn't get to just watch."

"Of course."

Erin eyed the older woman warily. "What did you have in mind?"

"I thought one of the costume- and mask-making workshops would be perfect."

Erin shifted uneasily on the swing. "You mean you want me to be in the parade." She moved again, looking for all the world like she was sitting on a bed of nails.

"Yes, I think it would be a wonderful experience for you to be in the parade. Then, after the ceremony, you could hang out with some of the musicians and dance."

"Dance," Erin spluttered, "you've got to be kidding." She bolted out of the swing and began pacing. She finally came to a stop, with her hands on her hips, in front of Evangeline. "I hate to dance," she announced finally, stamping one foot on the ground for emphasis.

With a twinkle in her eye, Evangeline murmured, "Yes, just the right energy."

"What's that supposed to mean?" Erin glared at the older woman.

"Why, just look at yourself, child. You're full to the brim with passion."

"You call this passion? I'm scared and upset, and angry . . ."

"Yes, indeed. Passionate just about sums all that up."

"I always thought of passion as something positive, exciting . . ."

"But you are excited," Evangeline interrupted.

Erin grew still. A moment later she said, "You're talking about intensity, aren't you?"

Evangeline nodded. "Why don't you like to dance, Erin?"

Erin grimaced. "It's another Jonathan story." Remembering her promise of Spring Equinox, Erin continued. "I guess I'm not being mean to him if I just tell you what happened. Months ago we were starting to learn how to dance in school. We had to change partners after each dance, and I noticed Jonathan watching me and trying to get

close enough to me to be my partner. I kept moving away, but he finally managed it. We started to waltz, and I kept looking away; I didn't want to look him in the eye. I ended up stepping on his foot, and he asked if I was trying to cripple him. I felt like he was saying I was heavy enough to do some damage, besides being a bad dancer. And when he wouldn't stop, I just got more and more upset and confused until I couldn't do anything right. It was awful." Erin sighed deeply, and slumped down onto the ground.

"Do you like to waltz?"

"After that? Of course not!"

"How about before that?"

Erin closed her eyes and rocked back and forth. "I don't honestly remember. What difference does it make, anyway?"

Evangeline slowly got up from the swing and extended her hand to Erin. "None, actually."

Erin grabbed hold and stood. "So I don't have to dance?"

"Of course you do." Evangeline laughed and drew a reluctant Erin along into the house. "Let's call now and get you into a workshop."

Three weeks later, Erin modeled her Mayday costume in her living room for Evangeline, Sarah, and her mother.

"Oh, Erin, it's lovely."

"You really did a nice job, Honey."

"It looks just like a spring flower garden."

Erin beamed. "That's exactly what I pictured as I made it—Evangeline's garden." Excitedly, she turned around again, showing off the skirt of yellow, orange, red, purple, black, and periwinkle.

"But what about your mask?"

"Oh, that's a surprise. Nobody gets to see that until the parade."

Sarah hugged her. "Well, I for one can't wait to see you in that parade."

"Nor I," said her mother, smiling broadly. "You're just beautiful," she added.

"And I can't wait to see you dance," said Evangeline. "Why, that skirt is just made for dancing."

Hoping no one but Evangeline could see, Erin spun to face the old woman. She stuck her tongue out quickly, then grinned, and turned back to face her mother. Evangeline began to laugh heartily.

On the day of the parade, Erin joined the others from her workshop at the park from which the parade would start. Everyone complimented each other on how they looked. Erin was proud to be one of them; each person had created a costume that was uniquely them, yet perfect for Mayday. One was a snake, another was an owl; she was the only white tulip growing out of a garden of color. She was so excited, she couldn't stop moving, hopping from one foot to another.

Finally, their workshop leader came by, announcing that it was their turn to start. The next thing Erin knew, they were marching down the street behind a percussion band made up of congas, rattles, a tambourine, a flute, and some other instruments Erin didn't recognize. But her body seemed to recognize the beat, for she found herself moving easily, bobbing this way and that, and even spinning occasionally.

"Isn't this great?" asked one of the other kids, obviously as taken with the music as Erin. Erin nodded, looking around, noticing that one or two kids were struggling with the rhythm, but most were flowing with it like they had been doing it all their lives.

After that, Erin totally relaxed and let the music carry her down the street. She was vaguely aware when she passed Rachel, and later her family; she could feel their voices cheering her on. Once she felt a brief uneasiness when she caught sight of a sandy head of hair, but she just danced it away, feeling totally safe behind her mask.

When they got close to the end of the route, and everything was slowing down, Erin felt sad and disappointed. She looked around and spotted her family camped out on the hillside with a perfect view of the upcoming ceremony. Somewhat reluctantly she joined them.

She accepted their compliments, then turned to Evangeline. "I like to dance, I really like to dance." Her voice trembled with surprise. "And I'm good at it, it comes naturally. It's the music, isn't it?" When Evangeline just smiled, Erin threw her arms around her and whispered, "Thank you," then turned her attention to the sun-welcoming and birth of the flowers. Then it was time to dance once more.

By the time Erin found her group, the music had started and many people were already dancing. Erin was relieved; she had not been looking forward to being extremely visible, no matter how safe she felt behind her mask, no matter how excited she was about her newfound love for dance. She moved into the group of dancers, weaving easily in and out, occasionally picking up a partner, then dancing away again.

One boy in particular drew her attention. He was in a peach and purple costume, two of her favorite colors, and he was dancing with great abandon. Erin wished that she could be that free. Before long, the boy had danced his way over to her and began inviting her to dance with him, pantomiming his intentions, and mirroring some of her movements. She followed suit, and found herself dancing more and more wildly. She began swaying her hips and swinging her head around, describing crazy eights in the air with her flaxen hair. Once again she became lost in the music. Vaguely she sensed Evangeline spinning her way through the throng. Again there was a moment of dis-ease when she noticed the boy's brilliant blue eyes, but the music wouldn't let her go for long. Besides, this boy obviously liked the way she danced. It didn't occur to her that it might be because she was dancing differently. Finally, the rhythm reached a frenzy, crested, then slowly diminished and came to rest in a rich silence.

Erin came to slowly, and looked about for her partner, who had disappeared back into the crowd.

As she took off her mask to wipe away the per-spiration, Erin heard a whoop. Turning toward the sound, Erin was engulfed in a bear hug by a breathless Rachel. "Oh, Erin, you were so beautiful, so graceful. I just knew it was you in that skirt. Thanks for telling me about this celebration, my whole family liked it." Before Erin could respond, Rachel, too, was gone.

Later that day, Evangeline and Erin sat by themselves under a tree, sipping water and watching the festival wind down.

"You want to know what I learned," Erin said matter-of-factly. "There is so much, I don't know where to start, how to organize it."

"Then I'll help you," said Evangeline. "Focus on your body. What did it learn? How does it feel?"

Erin closed her eyes and breathed deeply, as Evangeline had taught her. Without opening her eyes, she began to speak. "I feel like every part of me is on fire. I feel like something is waking up, I'm waking up. I feel . . . oh, this doesn't make any sense."

"Don't censor it, Erin, just say what you see or feel, in whatever words seem right."

"Okay, I feel this empty space deep inside me filling up. It's sort of like a well, but not really." She opened her eyes. "Do you know what it is?"

Evangeline turned her head to look at the last dancers on the lawn below them. "It doesn't matter what I know, Erin. It's for you to know or to find out." Without turning, Evangeline placed her hand on Erin's. "And I'd say you're doing just fine."

Midsummer's Eve

School was out for the summer before Erin saw Evangeline again. Erin arrived at the old woman's house on her bike, which she rode up the driveway to the back yard.

"I thought I'd find you out here," Erin said, laying the bike down. She strode over to where Evangeline, in a now-familiar bright orange sun dress and wide-brimmed hat, was weeding her garden. Erin plopped herself down on the grass and absentmindedly started pulling up dandelions.

"I appreciate your help, but it only works if you get them by their roots," Evangeline said, handing Erin a special tool for the purpose and then turning back to her work.

Erin likewise fell silently to her task. An hour later she set down the tool and drew her right arm across her sweaty forehead, leaving a streak of dirt. "I've pulled out dozens of dandelions, and I haven't moved. This task is endless and summer hasn't even started."

"This is summer, honey, no matter what the calendar says. Summer is tending to what you've planted that is now growing, making sure it has every chance of maturing."

"It's not very exciting," Erin replied.

"No, it's not," agreed Evangeline. "It doesn't have either the thrill of expectation and newness of Beltane, nor the sweetness of success of Lammas. It's the nuts and bolts, the bones, the long middle. That's summer," she finished, setting down her own weeding tool. "And it's thirsty," she added, making her way to the outside faucet where she turned on the sprinkler for the garden. As she headed for the back door she yelled over her shoulder, "I'll get us some lemonade."

A few minutes later, Erin and Evangeline sat sipping their cold drinks in the shade of a tree. "So what is the next ritual about?" Erin asked.

"Summer Solstice?" Evangeline pondered. "It's all about what we've been talking about . . . tending to what you've planted in your garden."

"Meaning my heart," Erin replied.

Evangeline nodded.

"Well, let's see," said Erin. "With Imbolc it was inspiration and paying attention to what was going on in and around me. With Spring Equinox it was about balance and making the bird sanctuary, or my heart, a welcoming place. Then, at Beltane, it was about passion and dancing with life rather than struggling against it. I'm trying to see a pattern or a common thread here, but it's escaping me." Erin remained silent for a time.

Finally, Erin spoke again. "Well, there is a common element, though I hate to mention it."

"And what is it, Erin?"

"Well, Jonathan. I've talked with you about him in preparing for each ritual so far. At Imbolc I was just plain mad at him; at Spring Equinox I was able to see some similarities between us; at Beltane he was part of my learning to dance, although I didn't particularly like how it worked with him." Erin paused again, struggling for the right words. "I didn't tell you this before, but I actually wondered if he was dancing at the Mayday celebration behind one of the masks."

"What if he was?"

"Then I really wouldn't know what to think, except that then I might be interested in tending to that relationship this summer."

"Does Jonathan need to have been one of the dancers for you to bother with him?"

Erin squirmed in her seat. "Ooh, I don't like the way that sounds at all, but we're not exactly friends."

"Okay, let me rephrase that. Do you and Jonathan have to be friends in order for you to learn from tending your relationship?"

"Well . . . I think I'm starting to see, but I don't quite get it yet." Erin knew she was being stubborn, but the thought of tending her relationship with Jonathan without a really good reason was difficult for her to swallow.

"Take my garden. I grow flowers because they are pretty, tomatoes because I like to eat them, marigolds because they keep certain things away from the tomatoes—probably because they smell so bad—bee balm because it's useful medicinally, and catnip because it's a challenge—if I can keep it alive, despite the neighborhood cats, then I'm tending my garden well."

"So, each plant, or each relationship I have, serves a different purpose, each one worth cultivating even if I don't like it a lot."

"Just so."

"I have the feeling that you're not going to tell me what to do this time—that it's up to me to decide, really, what my garden is and how I want to tend it."

Evangeline put a wrinkled arm around Erin, drawing a sharp breath as she did so. Before Erin could ask her about it, Evangeline said, "You still have much to learn, Erin, but what you have learned you have learned well, and you are quick to make leaps to the next step. It is a pleasure to teach you and learn from you."

Erin's eyes grew very big. "You, learn from me?" she stammered.

"Yes, indeed child, constantly." She would say no more.

The next day, Erin sought out her friend Rachel and told her about her conversation with Evangeline. "So, I don't know exactly what the relationship with Jonathan is about, but I know a lot about what our relationship is about. You're someone I can share things with without being afraid of what you might say, I have fun playing with you, and you got me interested in spending this year learning from Evangeline."

"How did I do that?" Rachel asked.

"Because you were so sure about your relationship with God, and I wanted to feel that way, too."

"And do you? You and Evangeline don't seem to talk about God."

"No, we don't, but I am starting to feel closer to Him or Her or whatever God is. Actually, I'm really feeling closer to myself and to the earth, which may be the same thing. It may be that what I am tending to now is my relationship with myself."

Rachel waited a moment before she replied. "All of that may be true, but I'll have to think about it because it's not quite the way my family looks at things. But I want to hear more about Jonathan. Are you actually going to go out of your way to talk to him?"

"Yeah. I don't exactly know why, but it feels important, like it's the right thing to do. Still, the mere thought of it makes me nervous. I was hoping you'd come with me." Erin glanced over at Rachel to see how she was taking this news. She had a look of pure astonishment on her face.

"You can't be serious, Erin. After how he's treated us? I can't believe you're actually considering it, even with Evangeline."

"Somehow I didn't think you'd be real excited about the idea," Erin said, a little smile playing at the corners of her mouth.

The next day, Erin went looking for Jonathan. She checked all the places she could think of where he might be: the schoolyard by the basketball hoops, the bird sanctuary, the kid's beach at the lake, the corner store, and finally his own back yard. It was with a mixture of relief and frustration that she stopped off at Rachel's house on her way home, but Rachel wasn't there. *Guess I am on my own about this one,* Erin thought, as she continued on home.

The next day was much the same, but this time Erin stopped at Evangeline's house on the way home. "Two days and no sign of him, can you believe it?" Erin finished her lament.

"Did you try knocking on his door?"

"Well, no. I suppose that would be a good idea if I don't find him tomorrow, huh? I guess part of me really doesn't want to find him."

The next day, Saturday, a more determined Erin approached the entrance to the corner store just as Jonathan came out, nearly colliding with her. "Well, well, look who we have here."

Before Jonathan could say any more which might melt her resolve, Erin blurted out, "Why, Jonathan, just the person I was looking for. Can I talk to you a minute?"

Erin noted with surprise and pleasure that for once Jonathan didn't have a quick, obnoxious comeback. "Why, sure, I guess, I mean, if you

really want to," he stammered. As Jonathan sat down across from her, a familiar sly look passed over his face. "Oh, I get it now, you probably want to ask me how summer school is going so you can make fun of me and lord it over me because you don't have to go. Well, you can just forget it, Miss Smartypants," he said, starting to rise.

"No, Jonathan, that's not it at all. I didn't even know you were in summer school. I really wanted to talk to you."

"Oh yeah, why are you so interested in talking to me now, huh?" Jonathan said, obviously suspicious.

"Well, to tell you the truth, I don't know exactly. I just thought it would be a good idea, since we keep running into each other and it never seems to be much fun for either of us. I thought if we talked we might be able to figure out why and straighten it out."

"You may not have much fun, but I have a great time. It's always nice to see you, Erin," Jonathan sneered.

But Erin wasn't sure anymore if it was the words or the sneer which was the lie. *He can be as stubborn as me,* Erin realized. Deciding she had nothing to lose at this point, Erin said, "I don't believe it, Jonathan. It can't be fun for you to tease people to the point where they hate you and never want to be around you. That would have to be pretty lonely."

Jonathan started to say something, then closed his mouth so tight Erin could see the muscles of his jaw quivering. She decided to continue. "I'm not saying that I want to be friends with you, because I don't know if I do or not. I haven't liked the way you've treated me or Rachel, or a lot of the other kids. But I don't like the way we, or I, have treated you, either, and I want that to be different."

Erin could sense that Jonathan was really struggling inside himself with what she had been saying. She even wondered if he would start crying, but he didn't say a word. She finally decided that the best thing might be to just leave him alone for now. Without saying any more, she stood up and walked away, not looking back.

"I was waiting for him to say something. I really wanted to know how he was feeling; I even wanted to help," Erin said, astonishment filling her voice. "Then I realized that, in some respects, none of that mattered; I had done what I needed to do, which was let him know what I had decided at Spring Equinox. That was what needed

tending. Somehow, deciding to treat him nicer was just the first step; I needed to let him know what was going on with me. I don't know what he'll do now, but I feel really good about myself in a way I haven't for a long time."

They were sitting on a bench in Evangeline's garden. It was midafternoon by summer standards, 4:19 P.M., on June 22. The sun was still high in the sky, filling the garden with light and warmth, bringing out the brightest yellows and oranges, and the deepest reds and blues in all the flowers.

"Today is the longest day of the year," Evangeline began. "The light, life, is in its fullness, but tomorrow it will begin imperceptibly giving way to the dark, death." Evangeline stopped a moment to pluck a petunia for Erin. Erin breathed in its fragrance, and drank in its nectar from the place where its stem had been. She then laid it gently in her lap as Evangeline continued. "You are tending yourself well, Erin; you are a beautiful addition to the earth's garden."

The two friends then sat quietly, watching the solstice sun slowly disappear behind the neighboring trees, leaving the garden in shade.

First Harvest

Erin and Rachel were in Erin's back yard, stretched out in lawn chairs, their feet dangling into a child's wading pool. "These raspberries are great, Erin," Rachel said, plucking another berry from the stainless steel bowl and popping it in her mouth.

"Mmm," Erin replied, as she sipped from her sweating glass of ice and lemonade. "They are part of my early summer harvest from the work I am doing with Evangeline. I go over to her place every day to pick berries for the two of us."

"That sounds like fun, especially after all the hard work you put in helping her weed the garden. It's nice that you get to share in the rewards."

Erin thought about this a while before responding. "Yes, it is nice, and fun, but it's not really any easier than the other work I've done with her."

"How so?"

"Well, I have to be careful to make sure each berry is really ripe and ready to be picked. If I wait one day too long they are already getting soft in this heat, but if I take them even one day early they don't taste very much like raspberries."

"Hmm," said Rachel, her mouth once again full of raspberries.

"A lot of the berries are low on the bushes, so I have to bend down to get to them," Erin continued. "After a while I can feel my back getting sore. And sometimes as I reach for a berry at the back of the bush I'll scrape my hand and arm on the thorns."

"Ouch, I forgot they have thorns."

"Mmm-hmm," replied Erin, her mouth now full of berries. After a few moments she continued. "Then each berry has to be checked for those awful little hard-shelled black bugs that bite. Did you know they bite?" Rachel shook her head. "Well, they do. Then the berries have to be carefully washed so they don't get bruised. The ones to be eaten fresh are set aside in a bowl, then the rest are dried and set out carefully, one by one, on a cookie sheet and stuck in the freezer. After they are frozen they are put together in containers and saved for winter baking."

"Wow," said Rachel, "I never knew there was so much to it. I thought you just picked, easy as pie, and then ate 'em."

Erin nodded. "That's what I thought, too. But I'm starting to see that the garden doesn't work that way; there's always something that needs doing, and it's never as simple as you first think. But . . ." she paused to put another berry in her mouth, "the way these taste makes it all worth while."

Early the next morning Erin was once again at her berry-picking task. She had learned quickly that it was best to pick before it got too hot, then do the work of cleaning and freezing in Evangeline's cool kitchen. That way she was usually done by 10:30, leaving her the rest of the day to do whatever she wanted. Some days Evangeline worked out in the garden with her, but more and more often now, like today, she stayed inside—even the heat of early morning being too much for her. But she was always in the kitchen, waiting for Erin with a glass of cold water or juice.

"Good morning, Erin. Another good picking, I see."

"Yes, it is," Erin said, setting down two cereal bowls, each filled to the brim with berries. "I keep expecting the berries to run out, but every day there are more, almost as though they're magic bushes."

Evangeline's eyes twinkled as she replied, "They are magic, Erin. Natural earth magic, that is," she said, laughing from deep down in her belly. Erin was always amazed at that laugh which was so big yet came from a woman who was so small.

"What do you mean, earth magic?" Erin asked, settling down into a chair, eager for one of Evangeline's lessons.

"Well, Mother Earth just knew that her children were going to love these berries like nothing else, and that they wouldn't be satisfied with one brief harvest like with strawberries."

Erin briefly recalled the two weeks of strawberry picking they had enjoyed earlier in the season.

Evangeline went on, "No, Mother Earth knew we would want more, so she made several different kinds of raspberries. They come in various colors and amounts of sweetness, but they also differ in when they ripen. There are early ripening bushes, which you are harvesting now. But you're already starting to see the flowers on the midseason bushes. And, just as you harvest the last of those berries, the early bushes will be producing a second crop, which will keep you busy into September."

"That's great! But why she didn't do that with strawberries, too?"

"I expect it's because strawberries are even harder to work with than raspberries and at some point people would just give up on them, wonderful taste or not."

Erin laughed, in total agreement.

On her way home, Erin saw a familiar-looking head of blonde hair in the distance. *Jonathan?* she wondered, feeling her insides tighten up at the thought. She fought to relax, reminding herself that their last encounter had gone rather well, at least on her end. With that, she picked up her pace, gaining confidence with each step. To her surprise, when they got within hailing distance of each other, Jonathan started to cross the street. *Not at all like Jonathan,* she thought.

Surprising herself, Erin called out to him. "Hey, Jonathan, how are you doing?"

Jonathan stopped, one foot poised to continue on across the street. Eventually he lowered it, turned, and stepped back up on the curb. He kept his hands in his pockets, head tilted down, eyes darting every which way, except looking at Erin.

"Uh, hi, Erin."

Erin was tempted to ask him why he wasn't being mean, but suppressed the urge. Instead, she held out her left hand with its raspberry-filled plastic container. "Have a raspberry. I picked them myself." As soon as the words were out of her mouth, she regretted them, sure that now Jonathan would have something nasty to say. But he didn't say or do anything. "Please, have a raspberry," she tried again.

Jonathan tentatively reached for a berry with his right hand. He looked at it for a long time before he finally took a bite out of it.

I wonder if he thinks I poisoned it, Erin thought.

Eventually Jonathan put the rest of the berry in his mouth and murmured, "Thanks, Erin, that was really good."

It seemed to Erin that neither of them knew what to do next. "Want another?" she asked, holding out the container once more.

"Ah, sure, I guess, thanks." Jonathan very carefully took one more berry. This one he quickly popped, whole, into his mouth. Again there was a tension-filled silence. This time, it was Jonathan who broke it. "We don't have any raspberry bushes. I wish we did; they're my favorites."

Erin was relieved to have a topic for conversation. "Actually, we don't either. I pick them for a friend of mine and she lets me keep half of what I pick."

"Wow, really? That's great. Wish I had a friend like that."

Again there was a pause, and it seemed as though it wouldn't end this time. But once again Jonathan spoke. "Who is it?"

"Who?"

"Is it Rachel?"

"Is who Rachel?"

"The friend who lets you pick berries. Is it Rachel?"

"No, it's not," Erin said slowly, feeling herself becoming cautious. She didn't want to say much to Jonathan about Evangeline for fear he might once again resort to making fun. She wasn't willing to risk that particular area of her life to his ridicule.

"Is it that older woman I've seen you with sometimes, like down in the bird sanctuary?"

Suddenly, Erin felt very exposed. She realized she still didn't trust Jonathan, not really. *Why should I,* she thought. *I've been scratched by his thorns lots of times, so it's good to be cautious, just like I am with the raspberry bushes.*

"Yes, it is," was all she would say.

Jonathan just nodded.

Encouraged by his timidity, Erin decided to take a risk. "She's teaching me things."

"What kind of things?" Jonathan asked, sounding sincerely interested.

Erin decided to take another risk. "Remember when we came back to school after winter break and I tried to explain about my family's Winter Solstice celebration, but I couldn't do it very well?" Jonathan again just nodded. "Well, she's teaching me about that."

"Good. Then maybe next time you'll know what you're talking about," Jonathan said quickly.

Erin turned a deep red, sorry she had said anything, sorry she had given him any raspberries, sorry she had called out to him. To keep herself from saying something nasty in return, she started to walk away.

He reached out a hand as though to grab her arm, then let it drop. "Erin, I'm sorry," he said. "I didn't mean it the way it sounded or, at least, the person I'm trying to be didn't mean it."

Erin paused and asked, "Just what did that person mean, then?" she couldn't help sneering.

Now Jonathan started turning red. "Well, gee, I mean, uh . . . what I mean is, uh, it sounded fun and interesting, and I was disappointed when you couldn't tell us more about it."

Erin couldn't believe her ears, but her heart told her Jonathan was telling the absolute truth.

"Really," he added.

"Well," Erin started slowly, "the truth is, I still don't know much about Winter Solstice. We've been taking the celebrations in order as we go through the year, and we obviously haven't gotten back to that one yet."

Jonathan bit his lip and swiveled slightly from his waist. "Would you, ah, that is, I'd sure like to know about what you've learned."

Erin gave this some thought. "Well, I guess I could tell you a little bit about Lammas, which is what I'm preparing for now."

"Okay."

As she talked, Erin made her way over to a little patch of grass where she sat down. Jonathan knelt beside her. "Lammas is about the first harvest, like these raspberries, which are the first food ready in Evangeline's garden. It's about the promise of that food, and the fact that so far it is only a promise

and not yet a reality. There's still a lot that could go wrong and make for a poor harvest. So, it's about celebrating the beginning and praying and then trusting that the rest will come out the way it needs to."

Jonathan sat very still, only his hands moving, playing with a clover. "That sounds kind of like our relationship right now. Like there's a chance that it will grow into something nice, but it's too early to know for sure."

Erin nodded, surprised by his quickness.

He extended the clover toward her. "It's got four leaves, for good luck. I'd like you to have it." As Erin took it, Jonathan jumped up, saying, "It's getting kind of late, I've got to go. Thanks for the berries."

Erin watched as he walked quickly to the corner, turned, and disappeared behind a house.

Two days later, Erin was recounting this to Evangeline over their Lammas picnic. Raspberries and cream, corn on the cob, butter, corn bread which they had made together, and a jug of grape juice were spread out on a blanket decorated with sheaves of wheat and a rainbow of flowers. "I never would have believed it, Evangeline, but

there's a chance that Jonathan and I could be friends." Erin reached for another piece of bread.

"That's what's so wonderful about life, Erin. In the middle of winter, who would think that the earth could give us even this," she said, sweeping her hand across the blanket and out toward her garden. "And now, we are poised on the edge of a huge bounty, but there is still no certainty about it. We won't really know until the time of our next celebration which way it will go. And by then, it will be over and we will be heading once more into darkness."

Erin picked up her glass of grape juice hesitantly, holding it slightly aloft and toward Evangeline. "So let us thank the earth, and the Goddess, for the bounty we do have, and celebrate with her the mysteries to come."

"Well said, Erin." Evangeline raised her glass to Erin's, they clinked, and each drank about half their glass of juice. The rest they poured back onto the ground as a further token of their appreciation. In silence, they continued their celebration of food.

Pruning

Erin ran up the steps to Rachel's house, flushed with excitement. Before she could ring the bell, Rachel opened the screen door. Erin grabbed her right hand and pulled her over to the porch swing. "I just came from Evangeline's. I couldn't wait to tell you. Our next celebration, the Fall Equinox, is going to be real different. She said it's so important to give thanks to the earth at this time of year, that we can't do it alone, so I'm to invite whoever I want. So I want you to be the first," Erin ended, out of breath.

"Ooh, that's great, Erin. Of course I'll come. Do I have to do anything special?"

"As a matter of fact, you do. This is a potluck, and a thanksgiving. So you need to bring some food, and it has to be something you make or pick yourself, made from something that grows here.

And you should be prepared to say something about what you are thankful for in your life."

Rachel began to pick up on Erin's excitement. "Oh, gee, Erin, there are so many possibilities, I don't know how to choose."

"Then bring them all! I certainly won't mind." Erin was notorious in her love for food, though to her friend's amazement she never seemed to gain any weight.

"Who else are you inviting?"

"Well, Mom and Dad and Sarah, of course. You're welcome to bring your parents. Actually, I'll invite them personally. And," Erin paused, unsure of what Rachel's reaction would be, "I've decided to invite Jonathan."

Rachel surprised Erin with her reply. "I'm glad, Erin."

"Really? I was worried you'd be upset and uncomfortable and maybe wouldn't want to come."

"I wouldn't miss this for anything. Besides, I can see for myself how different he is. I mean, we've been back in school for a couple of weeks now and he hasn't made fun of me once. I haven't gone out of my way to be around him, but at something like this, with adults around, he's likely to be on his best behavior, so it would be a good, safe place to spend a little time with him and see just how different he is."

Rachel looked right into Erin's blue eyes, then threw her arms around her and hugged her close. "I just think you're great, Erin. I'm so glad to have you as a friend."

Erin spent the rest of the day inviting the other people on her list to the equinox celebration. Rachel's parents were subdued, but sincere in their appreciation of the invitation. Her own parents were more animated and immediately started getting excited, just as Rachel had, about all of the possibilities for food and the giving of thanks.

Her godmother, Sarah, was next on her list. "Erin, what a pleasant surprise," Sarah said as she opened her front door. "Come on in, I was just making cookies and lemonade. Would you like some?"

"You bet," Erin answered, as she followed Sarah into the kitchen.

Sitting at Sarah's table, she noted some of the differences between Sarah's kitchen and Evangeline's. Evangeline's was white and, with its south and west windows, it was bright most of the day, even when the sky was cloudy. Sarah's kitchen was

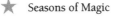

an off-white, with lots of light-colored wood, and a northwest exposure, so it was more subdued. While Evangeline's was always in disarray, looking like something was in process even when it wasn't, Sarah's, even in the middle of cookie-baking, managed to look as though nothing was happening. Her cats knew better, though, and sat expectantly near the stove.

"What kind of cookies are you making?" Erin asked, already knowing the most relevant part of the answer. After all, Sarah could always be counted on for a chocolate fix.

"Oh, those oatmeal raisin nut crunch cookies I love so much," Sarah said. When Erin's smile started to fade, she added, "You know, the ones with the chocolate chips in them."

Erin nodded and smiled, relieved. For a moment there, Sarah really had her believing there was no chocolate in them.

Just then the timer went off and Sarah pulled two cookie sheets from the oven. With a spatula, she removed the cookies from the sheets and placed them on plates. "I'll be right back," she said, disappearing through a swinging door into the living room. A moment later she came back with another plate in her hands, which she set down in front of Erin.

"These are cool. I have to put them in the living room to keep the boys from getting them," she said, nodding in the direction of the cats. A few seconds later she set a jug of lemonade on the table, along with two ice-filled glasses. She filled both glasses, took a cookie, and sat down next to Erin. "Mm, pretty good, if I do say so myself," she said, taking a bite from her cookie. "So, what brings you here today?"

Erin swallowed the bite of cookie in her mouth before replying. "I wanted to invite you to my celebration of the equinox with Evangeline. We both thought it would be nice to have a big potluck to celebrate the harvest. It seems like a good time to share with our friends, and that way we get more food, too."

"Very practical, as well as thoughtful," Sarah laughed. "Well, I am honored and grateful for the invitation. Is there anything else I should know about it?"

Erin explained the event as she had to Rachel, knowing that Sarah would understand the significance of everything. Then she thanked Sarah for the refreshments, gave her a big hug, and went to deliver her last invitation.

Erin had never been inside Jonathan's house. It seemed like a nice-enough house, with a neat, clean yard, but somehow it wasn't very inviting. It looks too neat, Erin thought to herself as she rang the doorbell. And all of the shades were drawn, even though it was only four in the afternoon.

A woman finally answered the door. "Yes?" she said, her mouth kind of pinched. In fact, the whole of her looked kind of pinched, from her feet in her small high heels to her hair, which was pulled back in a bun.

"Hi. Mrs. Tremont? I'm a friend of Jonathan's. Is he here? Could I speak with him?" Erin suddenly felt pinched herself.

"Jonathan?" The woman seemed to be studying Erin, trying to make a decision about something. "Why, yes, he's here. Just a minute." She began to close the door on Erin, then opened it again. "Who shall I tell him is calling?"

"Erin." This time the door did close, leaving Erin alone on the stoop. *Well, no wonder he's so uptight,* Erin thought to herself.

A few moments later the door reopened, and Jonathan joined her on the stoop. "Erin, hi. What are you doing here?" Jonathan looked back nervously at the door, which was once again closed.

"I came to invite you to my equinox celebration with Evangeline next Saturday." As Erin began to fill in the details, Jonathan grew more and more agitated, rocking back and forth on his feet. "Are you okay?" Erin finally asked.

"Yeah, I guess. I just don't know if I can come."

"Do you have something else planned?"

"No, I, uh, I don't think my parents would approve, that's all."

"They're welcome to come, too, if that would help. Should I invite them now?" she asked, reaching for the doorbell.

"Ah, no, uh, please don't. They, uh, they aren't big on religion anyway, and I don't think they'd understand about this, but if I just call it a party, maybe it wouldn't be a problem. But I have to bring something to share, huh?"

"It doesn't have to be a big deal, but yes, something to share is important." Erin realized that there was something very hard about this for him. Reaching out and touching his arm she said, "Look, whatever you bring will be fine, Jonathan. What's most important is that you come." After giving him directions to Evangeline's house, she backed down the steps and went home.

The following Saturday afternoon, Evangeline's back yard seemed transformed. A huge picnic table had mysteriously appeared, covered with a beautiful white tablecloth. Several vases filled with flowers sat on the table. Plates and bowls of stoneware were stacked at one end with stainless steel silverware and cloth napkins. Bowls filled with vegetables and dip appeared out of Evangeline's kitchen. Erin's contribution, a bean dip with corn chips, sat in the middle.

As the guests began to arrive, a gaily dressed Erin showed them where to put their gifts of food. "Over here would be great!" "There's a little room right here." "How about over there?" She could barely contain herself. When she had a moment, she drew Rachel aside and said, "Oh, Rachel, I never knew how happy I could be. This is so wonderful. I'm so happy to have you and your parents here."

Rachel was once again catching Erin's enthusiasm. "It is great, Erin. This yard is wonderful, with its flowers, and everything. The table with all the food looks terrific. And, I made the ice cream in Evangeline's freezer myself," she said proudly, adding, "Mom showed me how. What's that over there?" She pointed at a black kettle sitting on the ground in the middle of the yard's open space.

"Oh, that. Well, no feast is complete without a bonfire, but since we can't have one of those in

Evangeline's back yard, we settled for one made of Sterno. We'll light it later, as the sun is setting.

Rachel looked around nervously. "So, where is Jonathan? Is he coming?"

Erin frowned. "I don't know. I think he wants to, but it sounded as though his parents might not let him. He also sounded nervous about having to bring something to share. I hope he comes, so you can really see how different he is."

At that moment, Evangeline, dressed in green, joined the girls. "Jonathan is the only one who isn't here yet, right?" Erin nodded. "Well, we could wait a little longer, but I think we should get started soon. People are hungry, there's a lot of food to be eaten, and then we have the ceremony to do."

"Well, I did say 4:00 P.M., and it's 4:15 P.M., so I guess we could start."

"Okay I'll ring the bell and then why don't you say a few words of welcome."

Erin began somewhat solemnly. "I invited you all here today to help me celebrate the fall harvest."

Out of the corner of her eye, she could see someone approaching from the direction of Evangeline's driveway. *Jonathan? Yes, Jonathan.* Erin could feel her heart, then her mouth, begin to smile.

"I want to thank you all for coming and sharing the gift of food, of thanks, but most of all, yourselves. I'm grateful to know every one of you," she beamed at Jonathan, and then at each person in turn.

As they started filling their plates, Erin made her way over to Jonathan. "I was beginning to think you weren't coming. I'm glad you did."

"So . . . am . . . I," stammered Jonathan. Looking at the table, he added, "Everything looks so wonderful. I didn't bring much." He held out a brown bag filled with apples.

"You picked them yourself, didn't you?" Erin asked.

"Yeah," Jonathan said, shifting on his feet. "I climbed Mr. Headley's tree next door," adding hastily, "I asked him first, though. He said it was fine."

"Good. Let's eat."

A little over an hour later, though there was still plenty of food left, people had eaten their fill and were chatting amiably. Erin noted happily that Rachel and Jonathan seemed to be comfortable with each other. She herself was hanging out with the one person Evangeline had invited, a man named Michael who was full of stories about all the traveling he had done. She couldn't be sure if they were true or not, but it didn't really matter. They were definitely entertaining, just as he himself was. He had this distinctive belly laugh, something like Evangeline's, and he seemed in disarray, much like Evangeline's kitchen. In particular, his hair stood on end, going every which way as though it couldn't make up its mind about something. Erin was laughing when Evangeline leaned over, saying, "It's time to light the fire and start the ceremony."

Suddenly, Erin was aware of how dark it had gotten. She was barely able to see Michael's face. She nodded to Evangeline, dug down in her pocket for the matches, and made her way over to the kettle with Evangeline. She struck a match and quickly threw it in the kettle, noting with satisfaction the immediate leap of flames which silenced everyone. Slowly they gathered around the fire.

Evangeline raised her arms and began. "It has been a good year and a good harvest. We have eaten our fill and there is much to be grateful for. Who would like to begin?"

Erin stepped forward and said, "I am grateful for the bounty of my friends and for the knowledge I am gaining about the earth and her seasons, and what I am learning about myself in the process." She stepped back, indicating she was done.

Rachel stepped forward next. "I am grateful to have a friend like you, Erin, with whom I can share such similarities and such differences without feeling like either of us has to change."

Rachel's mother stepped forward. "I am grateful to have a daughter who teaches me so much."

Erin's mother was next. "I am grateful to find community like this in the midst of a large city, and I am glad of my daughter's role in bringing us together."

One by one the rest of the celebrants stepped forward and gave thanks until only Jonathan and Evangeline remained. Erin knew that once Evangeline spoke, Jonathan's opportunity would be gone. She also knew that Evangeline would wait a long time. The silence grew incredibly deep.

Finally, just when Erin thought she couldn't bear it any longer, Jonathan stepped forward and said, "I am grateful to be able to call Erin a friend," and stepped back.

Erin knew if it were light enough to see him, Jonathan's face would be extremely red.

Now Evangeline stepped forward once more. "I am grateful to have had this opportunity to teach Erin what I know and watch her develop her gifts. I now bring this ceremony to a close, but the celebration may continue as long as people want to stay."

Evangeline lowered her arms, then moved over to hug Erin. "It was a beautiful celebration, Erin, and I enjoyed all of your friends immensely." Leaning on Michael's arm, she added, "I am tired now, so Michael will take me in. Stay as long as you like. Just put everything in the kitchen before you go and we can clean up in the morning."

After giving Erin a kiss, Evangeline and Michael slowly walked to her back door. Erin watched anxiously until they were inside. Then she went back to her friends.

The next day, bright and early, Erin was back in Evangeline's kitchen, helping with the clean-up from the night before. "I think I've got everything under control here now, Erin," Evangeline said, her arms elbow deep in sudsy water. "Actually, there's one last equinox task that needs to be done out in the garden, if you wouldn't mind."

Erin gratefully put down the dish towel and headed for the back door. "Great, I'd rather be outside anyway. What do you want me to do?" Her hand came to rest on the doorknob.

"Well, all the raspberries are in, now, so it's time to get the bushes ready for next year. That means pruning them back."

Erin stiffened. "You mean cutting part of them off? I've never done anything like that before. It's kind of scary. I mean, why can't we just let them grow? They seem to do okay at it."

"Well, of course, they do, but pruning actually does help the plant. The parts furthest from the roots are the weakest, but they require just as much energy to maintain, which takes energy away from the raspberries and makes it more difficult for the bush to produce them. So, we help it along by cutting it back. Not so much that it won't produce anything next year, but just the parts that are old and weak and kind of scraggly anyway. Mother Nature has ways of doing this herself, but I like to help her out with the raspberries."

"How does she do it?" Erin wanted to know.

"Well, for example, in the bird sanctuary. The older trees eventually die and fall over, which makes space for new shoots to start developing."

Erin smiled. "I get it. Now that I understand, I don't think I'll mind as much." She opened the door and started to step out. "There's so much to learn. I'm glad I've got you to teach me," she said as she closed the door behind her.

Saying Good-bye

Erin lay on her bed, cradling a pillow, crying. Rachel sat next to her, one hand on the small of her back. Jonathan sat on a chair at the end of Erin's bed. It was some time before anyone spoke.

"I can't believe she's dead," Erin finally said. "We were just at her house for equinox."

"I know," said Rachel.

"Yeah," said Jonathan, squeezing his knit hat in his hands. There was more silence.

"I'm really angry at her, you know," Erin said, drying her eyes with the tail of her shirt.

"You are?" Jonathan and Rachel exclaimed in unison. Jonathan shifted in his chair, and Rachel sat up straight, as though a bolt of lightning had just gone right through her.

"Yeah, I am. I mean, she made me promise to work with her for a full year, then she cops out. Without even saying good-bye," she sobbed, once more throwing her arms around the pillow in her lap. Jonathan and Rachel exchanged glances, but kept quiet. There seemed to be nothing to say.

Slowly, Erin's body came once again to rest. She pulled herself up and looked at her two friends. "I'm glad you're both here. It really does make it easier, although you might not know it," she said, laughing for the first time that day. "Will you two be at the funeral tomorrow?" she asked, a slight edge to her voice.

"Well, I didn't really know her," Jonathan began, but after looking over at Rachel who was frowning at him, added, "Of course, Erin, if you think it would help. Besides, I'd do anything to get out of school." This time the silence was extremely tense, until Erin threw her pillow at Jonathan, relieved to have something else to focus on besides her sadness.

The next day, after the funeral, Erin was sitting on her couch next to her godmother. "I know this was your first funeral, Erin," Sarah began, laying her right hand on Erin's left knee. "I also know Evangeline was very important to you, as she was to all of us. So, I'm wondering what you think of all this."

Erin turned her eyes, puffy and red from all the crying she had done, towards Sarah. "Well, I sure got to feel sad, but beyond that it wasn't very satisfying."

"How so?"

"Because there are a lot of things that I didn't get to say to Evangeline before she left, so I feel . . . oh, I don't know . . ."

"Unfinished, incomplete?" Sarah suggested.

"Yeah. I thought maybe I could say them to her at the funeral, but she wasn't there."

"Where did you look for her?"

"In the casket, of course, why?" Erin asked, her curiosity aroused by Sarah's unusual question.

"Well, you're quite right about that . . . she wasn't in that body," Sarah murmured, apparently lost in thought. Despite further questioning, Erin was unable to get anything more out of Sarah that day.

A few weeks later it was Halloween, a day to which Erin had always looked forward before. Now she felt only sadness.

"You know, Erin, I haven't heard you talking about a costume for tonight," her mother said, poking her head into her daughter's room. "What do you want to be?"

Erin sat on the edge of her bed, swinging her legs. "I can't seem to get interested in it, Mom. I think about dressing up as a Gypsy, like Evangeline had once suggested, and then I just get sad and angry again. This isn't what I expected to be doing on Halloween this year. Somehow that dress-up stuff seems real childish now."

"Would you feel differently if you knew that Sarah and I were going to do something special with you when you got back from trick-or-treating?"

"Do you mean that I get to go with you and Sarah and the others to your ritual?" The mere thought had Erin thunderstruck.

"No, Erin, you know you're not ready for that yet." Erin looked at the floor, the excitement draining from her face. "But Sarah and I talked it over and felt we should do something special tonight, just the three of us, since it will be the best time this year for you to talk with Evangeline."

"Talk with Evangeline?" Erin couldn't believe her ears. "How can I talk to Evangeline when she's dead?"

"Come with us and find out," her mother said matter-of-factly. "But first I expect you to go trick-or-treating with your friends. They'll be here any minute," she added as she left the room.

That was all the incentive Erin needed. Twenty minutes later she raced downstairs, just as Rachel and Jonathan appeared in their costumes. Erin complimented both profusely. Rachel, in her long flowing golden locks and peasant skirt and blouse, looked just like Rapunzel. Jonathan looked very dashing with an eye patch and sword. They, in turn, raved over the outfit Erin had assembled so quickly—a black leotard and tights, a black head scarf, multicolored scarves draped from her waist, and some smudges of charcoal dust on her cheeks.

The three set off with a lot of excitement, talking about their favorite houses that had the best treats. Erin realized that for once she didn't really care how much candy she got. The best part of the evening was going to be later, after her friends had gone home. Then her mother and Sarah would help her talk with Evangeline. The thought was so distracting that several times during the course of the evening she wanted to cut her usual route short, but Rachel and Jonathan protested too much.

When she finally arrived home at 8:00, Erin found her mother preparing for the evening's adventure. She was putting the usual assortment of candles, scarves, incense, and other paraphernalia into a sequined bag. "I'm not quite ready, Erin, and Sarah's not here yet. Why don't you go get changed? You'll need to wear something warm, since it's going to be pretty chilly by the time we're done. And wear something black. We don't want to stand out tonight."

Erin nodded and went up to her room. She took off her Gypsy outfit and began dressing for what lay ahead. She kept the black tights and added a black turtleneck, some black pants, and finally a black sweatshirt. She grabbed the rock from Evangeline's garden from a shelf and stuck it in her pocket. Then she went downstairs to the front closet and searched until she found some gloves and a hat. She sure didn't want to be cold tonight. She wanted to be comfortable and have plenty of time to talk to Evangeline. Finally she was ready, just as her godmother walked in the door.

"You look like you'll be plenty warm," said Sarah, as they hugged. "Are you excited about your first real Halloween adventure?"

Erin bobbed her head several times as she tried to catch her breath. "Yes," was about all she could finally manage.

"A little nervous, too, it sounds like." Erin nodded again. "Well, that's okay, it's always a little scary on Halloween."

"It's so weird, Sarah. Before, when I just went trick-or-treating, I was never scared. I mean, I knew all the ghosts I saw were just other kids dressed up, like me. But tonight, I wasn't so sure of that anymore."

"It's good to have some uncertainty, Erin, but we're all going to be just fine." Sarah gave Erin another hug, just as Erin's mother came into the room.

"You two look ready."

Erin and Sarah nodded.

"Well then, let's go."

With Erin carrying a blanket, and Peg and Sarah each carrying a bag, the three set off on foot. They were headed for the bird sanctuary where a tree was going to be planted in Evangeline's name the next spring. The journey was made in silence, with each of the three preparing mentally for the upcoming ritual. Erin, not knowing what to expect, merely concentrated on relaxing. She reassured herself that in the presence of her mother and godmother, who had been doing this kind of thing for years, she would come to no harm.

The entrance to the park was marked by a fence with a tall, turnstile type of gate. Instead of going right in, as Erin was used to doing, the three paused. Peg lit some incense, while Sarah asked for permission to enter. "Guardians of the night, of the underworld, we seek entrance to your realm. We ask your blessings on this journey, and a guide to help us on our way."

After a moment they heard an owl hoot on the other side of the gate. They took that as their invitation to enter. One by one, first Sarah, then Erin, then her mother, they passed through the turnstile into what felt to Erin like another world.

In fact, it was another world. Even though Erin knew this place like the back of her hand in daylight, the dark brought to it a sense of mystery and even foreboding. The wide, bark-covered paths she knew so well seemed like tightropes, surrounded by bracken reaching out bony limbs to ensnare her. The little sounds that, during the day, she knew to be squirrels and birds darting through the underbrush, now sounded like sinister, alien creatures the size of moose. And when the moon edged up over the tree-tops, it only served to cast wicked shadows on the trails. She reminded herself that she was with two powerful, grown-up women, but she couldn't stop her body from shaking.

Just then Sarah took a right-hand turn onto a path Erin doubted she would have seen even in full daylight. A few minutes later, they arrived at a small circle that had opened up in the trees. Sarah halted and the others stopped behind her. Peg helped Erin spread the blanket on the ground, then laid one of her fancy scarves over the center to serve as an altar cloth. Out of her bag Peg produced a candle, some more incense, and a bowl of water, which she placed in the center of the cloth. From her bag, Sarah drew two different kinds of fruit, a loaf of bread, and a bottle of water, which she also placed on the cloth. After Peg and Sarah did some preliminary work, meant to consecrate and make safe their circle, the three sat down.

Sarah picked up one of the fruits, and began cutting it open. Peg used this opportunity to explain to Erin what was going to happen. "Sarah is cutting into a pomegranate, the fruit of life, which is death. It will assist us in our journeys. We will each eat three of its seeds, then close our eyes and begin. I do not know exactly what you will experience, but I have some suggestions for you."

Erin nodded, knowing she needed those suggestions, knowing she was scared and uncertain, but still trusting her mother and Sarah to see her safely through this night.

"We have already passed through one gate, but you may want to imagine another of some kind. You can pass through it yourself, but since this is your first time, I would recommend that you invite Evangeline to cross over to you. What is the thing you think of first when you remember Evangeline?"

"Her smile," replied Erin.

"Then start with that," said Peg. "Imagine her smile, like that of the Cheshire cat. You remember him?" Erin nodded. "Well, then, start with her smile, and slowly fill in the rest of her, adding in such things as her smell, her laugh, until she is fully present and standing right in front of you. Then, begin a conversation with her by telling her what you want her to know. She will most certainly respond. Keep talking with her until you feel finished, complete. You will know when that is. Then let Evangeline go back through the gate. When she is gone, reach in front of you for the piece of apple that will be there. Eating of the fruit of death, which is life, will help you reorient to

this world. When you are ready, open your eyes and wait for us to join you. Do you understand?"

Erin nodded and looked down. Sure enough, there was a slice of apple in front of her. Sarah was handing her the three pomegranate seeds. With some trepidation, Erin put them in her mouth at the same time as Sarah and her mother. She bit down and savored the sweet tart juice that exploded from the seeds. She had tasted them before in salads, but this was a totally new experience. Suddenly she felt a moment of dizziness. She quickly scrunched her eyes shut, then relaxed and waited. She couldn't believe her eyes! Directly in front of her, it seemed, was a huge stone wall with a large, uneven hole in it. There was darkness beyond, but in the hole itself something shimmered. She had the sense of gauze. Looking closely, she realized it was a gigantic spider web of fantastic colors. She remembered, then, to call out an invitation to Evangeline. Then she waited.

What seemed like an eternity went by and Erin began to think that nothing was going to happen. Relief and disappointment both flooded through her. As her disappointment grew, Erin remembered her mother's advice to look for Evangeline's smile. Immediately it appeared on the other side of the web. A form slowly took shape around that smile, and then Evangeline walked through the web. Erin just had time to realize that the web had remained intact when Evangeline opened her arms and enfolded her.

"Oh, Evangeline," Erin cried. "I miss you so. I want you back in my life. I know it's impossible, but I still want it." Before Evangeline could respond, Erin went on. "I'm angry with you, too. You asked me to agree to work with you for a year, then you left before that year was up. How am I going to finish my work without you?"

"Oh, Erin," Evangeline said, stroking Erin's head and back. "I'm still here, aren't I? And we are doing Halloween together." Erin sniffed and nodded, but remained stiff in Evangeline's arms. "I know that's not a great answer, and I understand your anger. I did make a promise to you that I didn't really keep. But it was time for me to go."

After a few moments, Erin relaxed just a little and leaned back to look into Evangeline's eyes. "Like those raspberry bushes you had me prune. It's sort of like I was pruning you from my life." Erin let out a sob and held Evangeline close once more. "But why?"

Evangeline stroked her head again. "So that I could move on, and so that you could grow, just as you're doing."

Erin nodded, letting go of Evangeline to dry her eyes. All of a sudden she reached out for Evangeline's hands. "Wait, don't go yet, I haven't told you the most important thing. I love you."

Evangeline smiled. "I know that, Erin, I have always known that. It's something I treasure deeply wherever I am."

"Really?" Erin asked, incredulous.

"Why, of course. You had so many ways of showing your love that I can't begin to think of them all. But I think the biggest thing you've ever done to show me your love is to come here tonight, when you were scared. You were very brave to do this, and I will carry this memory with me forever."

With this, Erin felt complete. So she said, "Good-bye," and hugged Evangeline one last time.

"I'm always here if you need me," Evangeline said, adding, "I love you." Then she turned and walked back through the web which shook slightly but once again remained intact. A few steps beyond the hole, Evangeline disappeared from view.

Erin waited a few moments, feeling full and satisfied, yet slightly sad. Then she remembered the apple. With her eyes still shut, Erin reached out and found the fruit, which she placed in her mouth. Even before biting down, she once again felt dizzy, though it passed more quickly than the first time. She opened her eyes to find both Sarah and Peg looking at her. "Was I gone very long? At first I thought it was forever, but now it feels like no time at all. I thought sure you would both still be there."

Peg and Sarah smiled. "It's like that," said Sarah, "especially the first time."

"You were gone just as long as you needed to be," added Peg.

Erin nodded. "I said everything I wanted to say, but I still felt sad when Evangeline left and it was time to return. Will I ever see her again?"

"Of course, Honey," said Sarah. "I expect you'll see her often in your dreams."

"And, you know how to penetrate the veil to the other world now, so you can see Evangeline and talk to her anytime you like," added Peg.

"But what about the pomegranate seeds and the incense and Halloween and all of that," cried Erin. "Don't I need all those things to make it work right?"

Peg and Sarah smiled again. "Oh, that," said Peg. "That's mostly for show, to get you in the right frame of mind. Really you can do it anytime, anywhere. All you need is your own prop, something that reminds you of Evangeline, or this experience, or of the other side."

"You mean, like the rock Evangeline gave me from her garden?" Erin asked, reaching into her pocket and feeling the stone's reassuring presence.

"That's perfect," replied Sarah. "Now, let's eat. Talking with dead people is hungry work." With that, she broke off a piece of bread for herself and passed the rest around, followed by the bottle of water and the remains of the apple.

The Returning Sun

Erin ran up the snowy steps to her house and opened the front door. Breathless from excitement, she turned to watch as her parents freed the evergreen tree from the top of their car. As they carried it into the house, Erin checked once more to make sure the tree stand was in place in the corner of the sun room. A few minutes later the white pine stood, bare but stately, in its place of honor. The family ringed the tree, admiring it.

Erin reached out a hand to touch one of the branches. "It's so soft. I love letting its needles run through my hand. I'm glad we got it early this year so it can be bare for a few days before we decorate it."

Laying a hand on Erin's shoulder, Peg said, "Yes, it does look nice just as it is, but I really enjoy the preparations for decorating it. It really gets me in the mood for the holiday."

"Me too," Erin said.

That night, Erin was sitting on the living room couch next to her mother, putting the finishing touches on a string of cranberries. "Why do we call it a Christmas tree?"

"What's that, dear?" Erin's mother put down her book, yawned, then put an arm around Erin to give her a hug.

"Why do we call it a Christmas tree since we celebrate solstice?"

"Old habits die hard, Sweetheart," replied her mother. "Your father and I each grew up in families that celebrated Christmas. That included having a Christmas tree, which is such a lovely part of the Christmas ritual that neither of us wanted to give it up, but we haven't gotten used to calling it a solstice tree yet." Peg paused a moment, taking in Erin's silence. "Are you thinking about Evangeline?"

Erin nodded and, bursting into tears, put her head in her mother's lap. Peg just rubbed her back, letting her cry it out. In a few minutes, Erin sat up, then snuggled in close to her mother.

"It was Winter Solstice last year that started my work with Evangeline. It's really hard to think that she won't be here for this one, at least, not in a way that's easy for me to understand." Erin paused, then added, "Not that you and Sarah weren't great at Halloween, but it still wasn't the same."

"I know, honey. And this is sort of like graduation for you, too, so it would be especially nice to have her here. But, your Dad and Sarah and I have been talking about what to do, and we've agreed on something."

"What's that?" Erin asked, drying the last of her tears with a tissue.

"Well, we want you to invite Rachel and Jonathan and whoever else you'd like to be here for Solstice Eve so your friends can see what you do. How does that sound?"

Erin beamed. "Just great, Mom. I'm sure Rachel and Jonathan will be excited, too. Thanks."

After one last hug and kiss, Erin laid her cranberry string on the dining room table and went up to bed.

Two days later it was solstice. About 4:00 P.M., Erin came down from her room, dressed in a black skirt and yellow sweater. She surveyed the scene with approval. The tree stood, waiting, in the corner, surrounded by strings of popcorn and cranberries. With some pride, Erin thought of her four strings. Off to one side were candles, and ornaments from previous trees. Erin felt in her pocket for the ornament she had just finished. She couldn't wait to see everyone else's. Looking outside, Erin noted with pleasure that a light dusting of snow was being added to the few inches already accumulated. She also noted a mixture of subtle fragrances in the air: pine from the tree, bayberry from a scented candle, and frankincense from an incense burner.

Just then the doorbell rang, and in bustled Erin's godmother, carrying a bulging canvas bag. "Sarah," Erin cried, rushing to give her a hug. "I'm so glad you're here. I can hardly wait for things to start."

"Things are already starting, Erin," said Sarah. "See, the sky is dimming. The reason for our ritual is upon us. Here, help me with this bag and then we'll call your parents and get started."

A few minutes later, everyone was gathered in the sun room, watching as the sun set in the west. Although it had been hidden for some time by trees and houses, it seemed to everyone that they could tell the exact moment it set. There was a change in the quality of the light, and a sudden stillness in the air, as though the whole world was holding its breath.

"Now begins the longest night of the year," said Sarah, "a night so long that we are never altogether sure if the light will return or not. And so we gather together to honor the night, and pray for the return of the day, and the rebirth of the sun. Let us begin."

The four quickly set about preparing for the others who would soon be joining them for a potluck meal and the evening's ritual. Shortly after 5:00 P.M. the doorbell rang, announcing the first arrivals, which included Rachel and Jonathan. Erin shrieked with delight, said, "Happy Solstice," and welcomed them in.

Each in turn gave Erin a huge hug, saying "Happy Solstice" back.

Rachel stepped in, handing Erin a grocery bag full of food, gifts, and her ornament for the tree. She then started to take off her thick blue woolen coat and mittens.

"It is cold out there, but at least it's snowing," she said, stamping her feet to get the last of the powdery snow off her boots. She was wearing a green woolen skirt with a red and green knit sweater. "I didn't know what to wear to a solstice party, so I just went with Christmas colors." Looking around the room at the tree and cranberries and holly, she added, "I guess they'll do just fine."

Erin laughed, then turned to Jonathan, who hadn't even begun taking off his down jacket. His eyes were huge, and busy taking in all of the sights.

Erin playfully elbowed him to get his attention, saying, "It's just a party, Jonathan," to which Jonathan replied, "I've never been to a party like this before. It's all so simple, but cool at the same time. And everyone looks dressed up, but comfortable, too. I don't think I'm going to fit in," he added, as he removed his jacket to reveal a suit.

Erin felt badly, realizing she hadn't told him what to expect. "Why don't you just take off the coat and tie?" she suggested. Jonathan seemed much more relaxed after taking her advice, and the three of them joined the party.

By 5:30 the dining room table was laden with an incredible assortment of culinary delights, the centerpiece of which was a grilled turkey. The food was so delicious that people kept going back for more. It wasn't until 8:00 P.M. that people finally gathered around the tree. With Peg officiating, they began their celebration by decorating the tree. First the strings of popcorn and cranberries were hung in circles.

"We offer these strings of popcorn and cranberries as evidence of the light's bounty to us."

Next, twelve unlit candles were placed on the tree, one on the uppermost tip.

"These twelve unlit candles represent the twelve hours of night and the twelve hours of day; the absence of light and the potential of light."

Finally, the ornaments were hung on the tree. First, ornaments from past solstices were hung. Then the new ornaments, each handmade, were brought out. Erin gasped with delight to see the wonderful assortment of offerings to both the dark and the light. There was a sun made of straw, a moon made of pewter, a star fashioned out of a coat hanger, small bouquets of holly and mistletoe, an apple carved from a block of wood and painted shiny red. She herself had taken an old silk scarf, sewn on beads and sequins, filled it with frankincense and myrrh, and tied it off with a piece of ribbon long enough to suspend it from one of the tree's branches. She noted that Jonathan and Rachel had really gotten into the spirit of the thing, too. Jonathan had carved a bird-like shape from a block of wood and had painted the beak orange. Then he had attached feathers and two small currants for eyes. It was really quite extraordinary. Rachel's ornament was a hand-crocheted star, starched, and hung from yarn.

It was nearly 9:00 P.M. Solstice would officially happen at 9:07 P.M. Peg brought out a huge sheaf of extra-long matchsticks. "It's nearly time for the lighting of the candles. Let us take a few moments to honor the silence of the dark and gather our thoughts." With that, she put out the lights that had lit the room.

Despite the lights that through the windows could be seen around the neighborhood, the darkness in the room was intense and disturbing. Erin could almost believe that the sun might never shine again. After all, it had been setting earlier and earlier, and rising later and later. Who really knew if it would continue that trend or start coming back to its summer glory?

After several minutes had passed, Peg spoke again. "It is time. If we can trust what has happened for centuries before us to happen again, the sun has finally stopped in its journey away from us. For a time it will seem to hang motionless, neither moving away nor returning. But a few days from now we will notice that it stays longer in the sky again, as it begins to return to its summer place in the heavens. In the meantime, I light this candle and honor the darkness for helping us to see and appreciate the light from the smallest of flames."

After a few moments, Erin's dad picked up a matchstick. After lighting it from the one candle already alight on the tree, he lit another, saying, "I light this candle as a symbol of the sun that blazes within us all."

Next, Jonathan, with no hint of his earlier discomfort, came forward, and lit a candle. "I like the sun for its warmth in the summer that makes it feel so good to jump into a cold northern lake." Appreciative smiles appeared on all the faces in the room.

"I light this candle as a symbol of hope for the world."

"I light this candle to acknowledge the warmth that draws us together."

And so it went until there were only three candles left unlit on the tree. Rachel, somewhat uncertain, but encouraged by Erin, stepped forward to claim a candle. "I light this candle to celebrate my friend Erin, who teaches me with her light."

Erin, astonished by this acknowledgement, almost forgot what she meant to say. When she recovered her thoughts, she stepped forward to light the eleventh and last individual candle. "I want to acknowledge the light which Evangeline is, and her role in bringing us all together tonight." Smiling at Rachel and Jonathan, Erin stepped back into the circle of Sarah's arms.

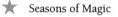

Then Peg asked everyone to pick up a matchstick and help light the twelfth and final candle at the very top of the tree. "Together we light this candle as a beacon, a guide for our sun on its return to us." Once the candle was lit, everyone stepped back to admire the tree. It seemed to Erin that there must be at least 100 candles on the tree, for surely twelve little candles could not shed so much light. Certainly the sun would have no trouble finding its way back to them with such a specter to show it the way. And certainly Evangeline had been drawn to their celebration, even though Erin couldn't see her.

Now it was time for Erin's favorite part of the celebration, the gift blanket. She had told her two friends that they were to bring an unwrapped gift for the blanket. It was supposed to be something of special meaning to them, so that the giving of it would be a kind of sacrifice. All the gifts would be placed on a blanket in the center of the room and, one by one, they would be claimed by someone. The turns were determined by passing a special stick around the group. The person with the stick got to choose a gift, say something about why they chose that particular gift, then pass the stick to someone else.

Erin's father called the group together around the blanket, the stick in hand. "I am going to let Erin begin this portion of our celebration, to acknowledge the work she has done this past year in learning about our celebrations."

Erin gasped as she accepted the stick, but quickly regained her composure. "I choose this yellow shawl because it is the color of the sun, and it reminds me of Evangeline. And, I pass the stick to Jonathan to welcome him into our circle." She leaned across the blanket and put the stick into Jonathan's hands.

Jonathan's voice trembled as he spoke. "I feel so welcome here tonight. And, in a way I have Evangeline to thank for that, but mostly I am grateful to Erin who worked hard at becoming a friend when I didn't give her much to work with."

Rachel, sitting next to him, playfully jabbed him in the ribs. Under her breath she said, "You mean, nothing."

Jonathan turned red, then reached for the leather pouch Erin had put on the blanket. "I . . . uh, I wanted something that Erin thought was special," he said hurriedly, shoving the stick at Rachel.

Rachel merely said, "This is every bit as beautiful and meaningful as Christmas, Erin. Thank you for inviting me," and she took a box of hand-painted note cards.

And so it went until all the gifts on the blanket were gone. As if on cue, everyone joined hands and began singing songs and swaying to their rhythm. They sang winter songs, and solstice songs, and Christmas songs they had been singing from childhood. They sang until the candles burned out and they were once again plunged into darkness.

After a few moments, Peg's voice broke the stillness. "We invite all of you who wish to do so to stay with us for the remaining vigil. We will sit up tonight, in the dark, talking, singing, chanting, drumming, dancing, waiting for the sun to rise. At its first rays we will gratefully break our fast with juice and scones. For those of you who need to go, we wish you a safe journey home, and thank you for sharing solstice with us."

Half an hour later, seven people remained in the darkened living room. Rachel and Jonathan had both gone, but only after thanking Erin and her family for a wonderful feast and celebration. Erin had felt proud to share her family's holiday with her two special friends. While some people sang softly, Erin rested her head in her mother's lap.

"Solstice isn't so different from Christmas, is it Mother?"

"Actually, it's not. But I'm curious, how do you see them as similar?"

"Well," Erin started, sitting up, suddenly full of energy again, "Christmas is the celebration of the birth of the son, s-o-n, the son of God. In celebrating solstice, we celebrate the rebirth of the sun, s-u-n. And it seems to me that both suns are about light and hope and energy coming back into the world."

"I couldn't have said it better myself, honey, and neither could Evangeline."

Erin smiled. "Evangeline was right."

"What about, honey?" asked Peg, putting her arm around Erin.

"She said that I would continue to grow and learn without her, and I have." After a few moments' silence, she added, "I still miss her, but she is so much a part of all of this that she'll never really be gone." Contented, she put her head back in her mother's lap and waited for the sun to rise. The only question in her mind now was, *What's next, what will the sun's return mean for me?*

Workbook

The Wheel of the Year

Shortly after the Winter Solstice which ended Erin's year of learning about and celebrating the seasons of the year, Erin found the following materials and this note among some papers that were left to her by her friend and mentor, Evangeline.

Dear Erin,

You asked me early on in our journey if I would write down what I am teaching you. I harumphed about it, because it's not in my nature to set things down this way, but . . . I did it! I hope you use these notes to continue developing your own understanding and celebration of the holidays we are sharing. Feel free to show them to any of your friends who are seeking a way of tuning in to their own and nature's rhythms.

Blessed be, Evangeline

General Notes

The holidays ("holy days") we've been celebrating allow us to honor the changes we notice both in the seasons of the earth and in ourselves. Although the things I've been teaching you reflect our European roots, these holidays are common to many cultures, including Native American ones, where the people are connected to the land, to earth. As you yourself noticed, these celebrations don't conflict with religious teachings because they are of a spiritual rather than religious nature. That is, they help us find meaning in our lives, and our place in the universe, without setting up strict guidelines for doing that. As I've told you, there is no one or "right" way of celebrating these holidays; it is important to celebrate them in ways which will bring them to life for you.

Because of when you came to me, we began by celebrating Imbolc, but you can start anywhere on the wheel of the year. It is called a wheel because the seasons, and life itself, are circular—there really is no beginning or end. Each holiday is associated with a specific date on which it is usually celebrated; on that date the season is at its fullness. However, each season is just that, a season or period of time, just like the twelve days of

Christmas, the eight days of Channukah, or the time of Ramadan, etc. That's why we began preparing for each celebration about three weeks before the holiday, then had our celebration on or near the actual date, and finally savored the season for the next three weeks, as we noticed how the season came alive for us.

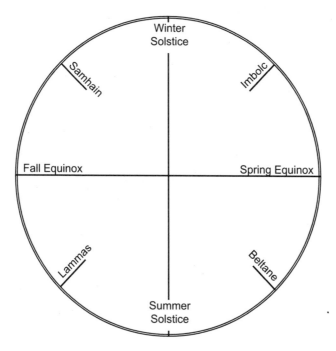

The Wheel of the Year

I am giving you two dates for each holiday just as a reminder that the season we are in depends on where we live. Since we live in the northern hemisphere, Winter Solstice coincides with Christmas, but for those who live in the southern hemisphere, where the seasons are exactly six months behind (or ahead) of us, it is Summer Solstice that coincides with Christmas.

Specifics

Hestia Altar

The Greek goddess Hestia is associated with the hearth—the fireplace where food was cooked and which was the center and gathering place of any home. A *hestia*, then, is a special place that is a center, or focus, of your attention. You've seen mine in my special room; I know you have one on a shelf in your room and your family has one in the dining room. You also know that we created one during each celebration. On them we place things that hold special significance for us in general, as well as things that remind us specifically of the meaning of the particular season we are in. This includes such items as: candles, pictures, rocks, feathers, and other items collected on walks or outings, bowls of water, incense, food, etc. My hestia is always changing, with some permanent objects, and many seasonal ones.

Containers

Wherever you celebrate, it is important that you feel comfortable and safe. Our houses naturally feel this way to us because of their familiarity and the walls that create a container for us, but there are certain things you can do to make any space feel this way. Thus, our celebrations typically begin with the creation of a "psychic" container, which is usually a circle within which the celebration will take place. We have created this circle in a number of ways: with a circle of people; by being in a natural circle of trees or flowers; by walking three times in a circle around the celebration space, sometimes sprinkling water or flower petals or cornmeal as we go; or by placing a candle in each of the four directions (east, south, west, north).

Invocation

Another way we have made the space feel safe is by inviting in, or "invoking," particular energies to be present with us as we celebrated. We have asked the Goddess to be present, our ancestors (special friends or relatives who have died), the energies associated with the four directions (East: air, spring, beginnings, the rising sun, the high-flying eagle, clarity of vision; South: fire, summer, the middle of things, the noonday sun, mouse, passion; West: water, fall, endings, the setting sun, buffalo, fluidity; North: earth, winter, the inbe-tween time, nighttime, the hibernating bear, intro-spection), etc.

Leader

Whether or not you create your celebration alone or in a group, it is often useful for one person to be responsible for the flow of the celebration from beginning to end. This does not mean that others cannot help out, or take responsibility for portions of the celebration, but it usually goes much more smoothly if everyone involved can look to one person to guide the overall flow of events. This offers an excellent opportunity for leadership and should be viewed as both a sacred and fun task. I know you felt a mixture of excitement and nerv-ousness when I had you take the lead, Erin, but I also remember how proud you felt when it was over.

Honoring and gratitude

Whatever else a celebration does, it honors us, the earth and its seasons, and whoever or whatever created all of this, so always make time for honoring and gratitude in your celebrations. We did this in a number of ways, including: silently, through meditation; physically, by the items we placed on the hestia; verbally, by having everyone take a turn at saying aloud what they were grateful for; through food, especially food associated with the particular season we were celebrating. I always save the food for the end of the ritual, because after eating we tend to become tired and unable to focus on the purpose of the celebration. Although it is important to eat the food mindfully and with reverence, this is also a natural place to be playful. I also like to fill an extra plate with food and set it outside where God, the Goddess, or their messengers—like an animal—can partake of the bounty along with us.

Closing the circle

I hope you have noticed that whatever energies we invite in at the beginning of our celebrations, we acknowledge, thank, and release at the end. And I always close the circle with the following chant:

*May the circle be open but unbroken; may the
love of the Goddess (or whomever you want to
mention here) be ever in our hearts; merry
meet, and merry part, and merry meet again.*

Although this is one of my favorites, you can
use a special poem or a chant that you make up
yourself.

Continuity

Because each celebration is, by nature, different, I
always like to have one or two things, like the
closing chant, which remain the same across all
celebrations as a way of maintaining a sense of
familiarity. I also like knowing that other people
around the planet are doing some of the same
things—it helps me to feel connected with all of
them. For me having a hestia is one way of doing
this, but there are many others. Though I don't
cotton much to book learning, I'm giving you a
list of books that may help you in developing this
kind of continuity (page 146). I've also written
down some of the questions I asked you to consider as we began our work together, and as each
season arrived. I think they were helpful to you
the first time around, and it might be interesting
to see if your answers are different each time you
move through the wheel.

The most important thing in this journey, Erin is to have fun, be joyful. Spirit loves fun! And that's what these celebrations are for, to honor Spirit.

Getting Started

Questions:

1. Why are you interested in celebrating the seasonal holidays? What are you looking for, hoping for?

2. God, the Goddess, Spirit; Jesus, Mohammed, Allah—these are some of the names that are used to refer to something that is bigger than ourselves—someone or something that guides our steps, answers our prayers, opens our hearts. To whom do you pray? Do you ever wonder about that One? Do you ever see that One in yourself, in others, in nature?

3. Many people go on journeys, either physically or within themselves, in order to find out more about themselves and their God or Goddess. These journeys can seem difficult, unusual, or even scary. (Just because something is scary doesn't mean it is

a bad thing to do; we are often scared simply because we don't know what will happen next, and we are sometimes scared by things we really enjoy, like roller coasters.) Are you curious enough about God/Goddess/Spirit that you are willing to do something a little scary or unusual in order to learn more?

4. Just as the earth has seasons, so do we. The obvious ones are: babyhood, childhood, adolescence, early adulthood, middle adulthood, and old age. But we also go through seasons within each of those seasons—times of success and failure, times of joy and sadness, times of plenty and scarcity. Are you interested in learning about your seasons? What kind of season are you in right now?

5. In order to celebrate the seasons properly, you have to give of yourself. One obvious sacrifice is some of your time, but you might have to give in some other ways. Are you willing to make some sacrifices in order to find out more about yourself and God/Goddess/Spirit?

Imbolc

(Candlemas, St. Bridget's Day)
February 2/August 2

The season of Imbolc begins three weeks after Winter Solstice (about January/July 12). It is traditionally associated with: the returning of the sun and light; the quickening of life, as in the birth of lambs; the color white; poetry and other arts and crafts; inspiration (breathing in); the Celtic goddess Bridget (patroness of poets and healthy babies; a healer); initiations (beginnings). In making your preparations, you may want to meditate on your breath for ten minutes each day.

Meditation

There are many ways of meditating; using your breath is one of the most simple. Sit still and pay attention to your breath as you breathe in and out, in and out, in and out, You may find your mind wandering, thinking about all kinds of things such as friends, homework, all of the things you'd rather be doing; if so, gently bring your attention back to your breath, and the rise and fall of your chest. When you are finished, you might want to make some notes about what you noticed.

Questions to help you focus on what Imbolc means to you:

1. The first three weeks following Winter Solstice (December/June 21) we don't see much change—we gain only sixteen minutes of daylight. Then the season of Imbolc begins and by Imbolc itself we gain another forty-five minutes of daylight. What can you do to pay attention to this, become more aware of this? What kinds of changes are happening in your body, your emotions, your thoughts —are they getting "lighter" as well?

2. Imbolc is traditionally a time of inspiration and poetry. What does Imbolc inspire in you—a poem of your own, or some other artistic or creative endeavor?

3. In Western/American tradition, Imbolc is acknowledged as Groundhog Day. This is the

day when the groundhog comes out of his lair and, depending on whether or not he casts a shadow, forecasts the length of time remaining in winter. How might this be related to Imbolc?

Spring Equinox

March 21/September 21

The season of Spring Equinox begins three weeks after Imbolc (about February/August 23). It is traditionally associated with: balance of all kinds, including hours of daylight and hours of darkness; movement toward greater light and less darkness; first signs of growth in plants and animals; daffodils and jonquils; dedication and naming of newborn babies; rebirth; the return from the underworld of Persephone to her mother Demeter. In making your preparations, you may want to take a walk outside each day, paying attention to any signs of spring and new life that might be visible.

Walking Meditation

Take regular walks around your neighborhood, looking and listening for signs of spring: fattening leaf buds on trees; green shoots foretelling the coming of the first flowers of spring; the first robin; the spring call of cardinals; people being outside more, making preparations in their gardens for things to come.

Questions to help you focus on what Spring Equinox means to you:

1. Besides sunlight and darkness, what other signs of "balance" do you notice at this time of year? (Look both outside and within yourself to answer this question.)

2. What could you do to welcome the signs of spring you notice on your walks?

3. Is there someone in your life who seems more dark than light in her/his makeup? Would you be willing to try and find more of their light? How can you do this? Does their darkness remind you of anything about yourself?

Beltane

(May Day)
May 1/November 1

The season of Beltane begins three weeks after Spring Equinox (about April/October 11) It is traditionally associated with: many flowers coming forth; passion; wild, untamed energy; blessing the fields; planting; bonfires; dancing wildly. In making your preparations, you may want to make a mask or costume that represents something you associate with the fiery energy of spring, which is coming alive in you right now.

Making a mask

This can be as simple as cutting up a paper plate and decorating it with crayons, glitter, feathers, ribbons, etc., or as elaborate as actually making a plaster cast of your face, which you then paint and otherwise decorate. (A local art store should be able to give you some tips.)

Questions to help you focus on what Beltane means to you:

1. What is on fire within you? That is, what are your deepest desires, fondest wishes, strongest dreams?

2. How can you bring out these dreams, giving them voice? (You could dance them, paint them, sing them, sculpt them, create a play with some friends, etc.)

3. As you consider this, you may find that you are nervous, fearful, or hesitant. What would help alleviate those feelings? Would you be willing to go ahead in spite of your fears?

Summer Solstice

(Midsummer)
June 21/December 21

The season of Summer Solstice begins three weeks after Beltane (about May/November 22). It is traditionally associated with: the fullness of the sun; the longest day; noon; the prime of life; love and marriage; endurance; fulfillment; roses and other later, longer-blooming flowers. In making your preparations, you may want to spend some time in a garden, whether it's in your own yard or a nearby park, observing what needs to be done, and helping out where possible.

Making your own garden

Ideally you would start a garden earlier in the season, planting seeds in indoor pots around Imbolc, or putting plants in the ground as soon as the threat of frost is gone for the year (after Beltane).

And, it would be nice to have a plot of land for this purpose. If your family does have land, perhaps your parents would let you be responsible for taking care of a certain part of it. If not, you can always plant seeds in pots, put them in a window, and watch them come up. A window assortment of herbs (rosemary, dill, oregano) is always a nice addition to the kitchen. Seeds, pots, and dirt are available at the local hardware store; just follow the directions on the seed packet.

Questions to help you focus on what Summer Solstice means to you:

1. What are you filling up with?

2. What are you tending in your physical garden and the garden of your heart?

3. Though there are some early rewards in gardening (lettuce, peas, a budding friendship), summer is generally about patience, endurance, and delaying gratification. How do you feel about waiting for things you want? Is it easy or hard for you? What makes it easier? (What little rewards now will help you stay interested until you can reap the bigger rewards later?)

Lammas / Lughnasad

August 2/May 2

The season of Lammas begins three weeks after Summer Solstice (about July/January 12). It is traditionally associated with: the beginning of the harvest; the goddess of grain, Demeter; mothers; bread; the honoring of food; gathering; nurturing; wisdom; meditation; patience; trust; yellow; corn; fairs. In making your preparations, you may want to help with the harvesting in your own or someone else's garden.

Harvesting

Picking does need to happen on a daily basis, so be sure you go out and take at least five minutes each day to look over what is ripe and ready to be picked, what is overripe and beginning to soften or wither, and what is not yet at its peak. Even if you don't have a garden, you can observe this in flowers as they begin to develop, reach their peak, then start to turn brown around the edges.

Questions to help you focus on what Lammas means to you:

1. What are you beginning to harvest in your life? (This can be in terms of food, flowers, relationships, work, creativity, etc.)

2. Do you trust that what you are just beginning to harvest will reach its full potential? What can you still do to try to ensure a full and complete harvest?

3. How can you celebrate what you have already gathered? Can you celebrate it as if it is enough, in and of itself?

Fall Equinox

September 21/March 21

The season of Fall Equinox begins three weeks after Lammas (about August/February 23). It is traditionally associated with: the harvest moon; nature in balance, but about to move into darkness; the fall harvest; celebrations of food with thanksgiving; prosperity; appreciation; brown; late-blooming flowers, such as mums; apples; abundance; pruning, to make room for next year's growth. In making your preparations, you may want to do some pruning of your own.

Pruning

Pruning can apply to many areas of our lives: our gardens, our toy chest, our clothes closet, the amount of food we eat, etc. Are there things in your closet, on your bookshelf, in your toy chest that you no longer use but that are taking up space that you could use for something else? If so, consider putting some of them in a box and giving them away to make room for something new, even if you don't know what that might be.

Questions to help you focus on what Fall Equinox means to you:

1. How has your harvest turned out? Has it been abundant or somewhat scarce? How does it feel to take notice of such things?

2. How will you plant your garden next year? Will you plant the same things, or try something new?

3. Is there some way of storing up your abundance for the winter that lies ahead?

4. How do you feel about pruning? Is it a difficult or easy task?

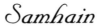

Samhain

(Halloween)
October 31/May 1

The season of Samhain begins three weeks after Fall Equinox (about October/April 12). It is traditionally associated with: death; ancestors; the time of year when the veil between the worlds of the living and the dead is the thinnest; the goddess Hecate, who sits at the crossroads of life, giving directions; barren fields; the first taste of the coming cold of winter; the Celtic new year; letting go; remembering; preparing for winter. In making your preparations, you may want to think about people/ancestors who have died or in some other way left your life.

Ancestor collage

Ancestors can be blood relatives, friends, mentors, mythical heroes from your cultural myths, etc.

You might want to make a collage of your ancestors for your Samhain hestia. This can include photographs, symbolic pictures, and words.

Questions to help you focus on what Samhain means to you:

1. Have you experienced the loss, through death or some other means, of someone special in your life? If so, how do you feel about them leaving? If not, how do you feel about the "death" of the earth or your garden at this time of year?

2. Consider your ancestors. Is there one in particular with whom you would like to speak, if you could? What would you like to say to them? Is there something you would like to know or hear from them? Can you imagine talking with them about this? (Ancestors remain very much alive in our imaginations; try having a conversation with one, or write a letter to them in your journal.)

Winter Solstice

(Yule)
December 21/June 21

The season of Winter Solstice begins three weeks after Samhain (about November/May 21). It is traditionally associated with: the longest night of the year; the hope of the return of the sun and light; rebirth; introspection; renewal; the pine tree; poinsettia, holly, mistletoe; frankincense, myrrh. In making your preparations, you may want to think about how you might like to invite light, hope, and energy back into the world and your life.

Making a solstice ornament or decoration
Consider what represents light, hope, and energy for you, and turn that into some kind of ornament or decoration for a tree, a window, or your solstice hestia.

Questions to help you focus on what Winter Solstice means to you:

1. Does your family have another holiday you traditionally celebrate at this time of year (Christmas, Channukah, Kwanzaa, or other occasion)? How is that celebration like Winter Solstice?

2. What are some of the things that provide light in your life? (These can be physical, like candles, or nonphysical, like friendships.)

3. What can you do to make sure that you always have light in your life or that, after a period of darkness, it returns?

Sample Worksheet for a Lammas Celebration

Holy-day: *Lammas*

Date to be celebrated: *Aug 2*   Year: *1997*

Hours of daylight: *14½*

Hours of darkness: *9½*

Participants/ guests: *me, Mom, Dad, Bobby (brother), Cindy, Angelina*

Location (indoors/outdoors): *Winona State Park*

What is the weather like? *generally sunny, dry*

Things you enjoy doing at this time of year: *going to county fairs, getting ready for school to start, going to the beach, eating corn on the cob*

What do they have to do with this celebration? *fairs: crops/prizes/celebrate; corn: being harvested; school: the end of summer; beach: fun*

Items to be found or made and placed on the "hestia": *an ear of "Indian" corn, a cornucopia, a green candle, fresh flowers, a recipe for veggie stew*

Who is the overall leader of this celebration? *ME!*

How will you create your circle? *with cornmeal and burned sage*

Who will do this? *I will do the cornmeal, Bobby will do the sage*

What energies will you invoke at the beginning/who will do it? *Mom, East: rising sun inspiration, beginnings (our first celebration); Dad, South: fire, passion, excitement, enthusiasm, happiness; Cindy, West: setting sun, the end of summer, food; Angelina, North: darkness, time alone, quiet, peacefulness*

What is the main point you wish to make with your celebration/what do you wish to honor? *the summer that brings us so much of what we love, especially food (corn, tomatoes, carrots, potatoes, onions, beans)*

How do you want to do this? *have each person bring something to put into a stew which we can all eat together; bless the ingredients and the stew*

What objects/props will you need to do this? *a fire, a large pot, water, herbs, other ingredients; our hestia, eating utensils; sage; cornmeal*

What needs to be made ahead of time? *the cornucopia; soup stock*

What foods are available/appropriate for this celebration? *corn, tomatoes, carrots, potatoes, onions, beans (fresh and dried)*

How will you end/close the circle? *a poem I wrote with Mom*

Suggested Worksheet for Each Celebration

(Please feel free to copy this sheet.)

Holy-day _____

Date to be celebrated: _____Year_____

Hours of daylight: _____

Hours of darkness: _____

Participants/guests: _____

Location (indoors/outdoors): _____

What is the weather like? _____

Things you enjoy doing at this time of year: _____

_____

What do they have to do with this celebration?

_____

Items to be found or made and placed on the "hestia": _____

Who is the overall leader of this celebration? ___

_____

How will you create your circle? _____

Who will do this? _____

What energies will you invoke at the beginning/ who will do it? _____

_____

_____

_____

What is the main point you wish to make with your celebration/what do you wish to honor? ___

_____

How do you want to do this? _____

_____

What objects/props will you need to do this? ___

_____

What needs to be made ahead of time? _____

_____

What foods are available/appropriate for this celebration? _____

_____

How will you end/close the circle? _____

_____

Notes:

_____

_____

_____

_____

_____

_____

_____

_____

_____

_____

_____

Follow-Up Worksheet

(To be filled out in the two to three weeks following the celebration)

What changes have you noticed in yourself since the celebration? _____

_____

_____

What did you like about the celebration? _____

_____

_____

What didn't you like? _____

_____

What would you definitely like to repeat in the next celebration? _____

_____

In next year's celebration? _____

_____

What would you definitely change, and how, in the next celebration? _____

_____

In next year's celebration? _____

_____

Is there someone who was missing from this celebration whom you would like to invite to the next one (or next year)? _____

Suggested Reading

Campanelli, Pauline. *Wheel of the Year: Living the Magical Life*. St. Paul: Llewellyn Publications, 1989.

Johnson, Julie Tallard. *The Thundering Years: Rituals and Sacred Wisdom for the Journey into Adulthood*. Bindu Books, 2001.

Morrison, Dorothy. *Yule: A Celebration of Light & Warmth*. St. Paul: Llewellyn Publications, 2000.

RavenWolf, Silver. *Halloween*. St. Paul: Llewellyn Publications, 1999.

Starhawk. *Circle Round: Raising Children in the Goddess Tradition*. New York: Bantam Books, 1998.

Starhawk. *The Spiral Dance: A Rebirth of the Ancient Religion of the Ancient Goddess*. San Francisco: HarperSan Francisco, 1999.

Svien, Kaia. *To Follow the Moon*. Lakeville, Minn.: Galde Press, Inc., 1999.

Glossary

altar: a place used to focus one's attention and acknowledge one's connection to Spirit; often a special cloth upon which one puts objects (such as feathers, stones, crystals, pictures) which remind one of their connection to Spirit.

Beltane (Mayday): May 1; traditionally the time of blessing the fields so that the crops being planted will grow well; also the time to celebrate the passionate side of life.

blessing: a gift of some particular quality which comes to one easily.

ceremony: a ritual; a time to honor a specific aspect of one's connection to Spirit, such as a birthday, an anniversary, or a season.

Cheshire cat: a character in Alice in Wonderland that, like Evangeline, is trickster-like (in its ability to appear and disappear) and is known for its great smile, which is the first and last thing you see of it.

circle: a sacred shape that has no beginning and no end, and within which one can safely perform ceremonies/rituals.

conga: a type of drum often used in ceremonies for encouraging dancing with total freedom.

consecrate: to make holy or special.

crystal: often used in rituals/healings to focus particular types of energy; for instance, rose quartz is usually associated with love.

cultivate: to grow or nurture.

Demeter: the Greek goddess of wheat/harvest.

earth festival: a time when a particular quality of "earth magic," is celebrated; in particular, Samhain, Winter Solstice, Imbolc, Spring Equinox, Beltane, Summer Solstice, Lammas, Fall Equinox.

earth magic: the magic inherent in life and living things, such as Gaia.

Equinox, Spring/Fall (vernal/autumnal): those two times of year (March 21/September 21) when the Earth is in balance, when the amounts of light and darkness are about equal in a single day.

funeral: a ceremony to acknowledge the passing of a particular person/spirit from life to another realm of being.

Gaia: a name for Earth which acknowledges that Earth herself is a conscious, living being.

gate: a passageway from one realm to another.

gift blanket: a traditional way of exchanging gifts.

God: a male representation of the Divine energy which created the universe.

god or goddess mother/father: a person who is responsible for the spiritual development of a child; never one of the birth parents.

Goddess: a female representation of the Divine energy which created the universe.

guardian: one who looks out for another, keeping them safe; can be human, but is often a spirit.

Gypsy: a member of a roaming group of people who originated in northern India and Egypt, and now living chiefly in Europe.

Halloween (see Samhain).

harvest: a time to pick the fruits of one's labors; this can refer to an actual food, or a quality which one has been developing in oneself.

Imbolc: February 2; a time of initiation, of celebrating the growing and visible return of the sun into our lives.

incense (like bayberry, frankincense): usually an herb which is burned to release its scent which has a particular healing or magical quality; for instance, sage is often used to cleanse and purify.

initiation: to consecrate one's entry into a particular aspect of life; in Christianity, confirmation is initiation into adulthood (this is known as Bat or Bar mitzvah in Judaism).

inspiration: literally, to "breathe in"; to open oneself to the creative energy of Spirit.

Lammas: August 2; the time of first harvest when we celebrate the picking of the first fruits of the field which was planted in spring.

Mayday (see Beltane).

meditation: a way of focusing one's energy inward to connect with Spirit; this is often done by paying attention to one's breath, or watching the flame of a candle.

Midsummer's Eve (see Summer Solstice).

mystery: something that is unknown, but affords unlimited possibilities.

owl: a winged creature, often associated with wisdom and seeing in the dark.

paraphernalia: tools (such as an altar cloth, feathers, crystals, incense) that help one to consecrate one's rituals.

passion: the fire or enthusiasm which brings anything to life.

Persephone: as Kore, she is Demeter's daughter; as Persephone, she is "Queen of the Underworld."

pomegranate: a fruit made of seeds, three of which, when eaten, kept Persephone in the underworld.

prune: to cut back so as to help growth.

Rapunzel: a fairy tale character who was known for her long, blonde hair, which the prince used to climb up to meet her in her tower room.

realm: an energetic "layer" of the universe.

religion: a way in which a particular group of people have developed to celebrate their connection to Spirit; examples include: Wicca, Christianity, Judaism, Islam.

resolution: resolve or intention.

sacred: holy.

sacrifice: something one "gives up" or exchanges for something else.

Samhain (Halloween or All Hallow's Eve): October 31; the time when the "veil" between the realms of Earth and Spirit is thinnest.

sanctuary: a safe space.

spider: an insect (*arachnid*) known for its ability to weave; symbolizes the Creator (weaver of the universe) in certain cultures (especially some Native American tribes).

Spirit: another name for God or Goddess; a realm of life which is less solid than that on earth.

Summer Solstice (Midsummer's eve): June 22; that time of year on Earth when things, including hours of daylight, reach their fullness and begin the journey once again toward darkness and death.

thanksgiving: a time or way of expressing gratitude for one's gifts, including the food on one's table.

Trickster: that aspect of life (known in some Native American tribes as "Coyote") that plays unexpected tricks on us, which usually help us along our journey, even though we don't understand or like it at the time.

underworld: another name for "spirit realm"; in Greek mythology it is the place where people go when they die.

veil: something that separates two things; can be thin and see-through, or thick and dense.

vigil: keeping watch for something.

Winter Solstice: December 21; that time of year on earth when things, including hours of daylight, are at their low point, just as they begin the journey once again toward light and life.

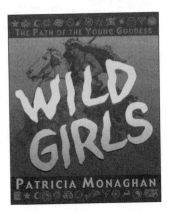

Patricia Monaghan

Wild Girls:
The Path of the
Young Goddess
*Twelve Inspiring
Stories of the
Maiden Goddess*

Maiden, Mother, Crone. Of the three faces of the goddess, the maiden corresponds to the part of a woman's soul that is always questing, always free to move and explore, always free to follow her own heart. She is among the most loving and giving—and heroic—of the goddess images.

She is the Wild Girl. Like natural wilderness, she lives by her own laws. And she is part of all women—from preteens who are just beginning their path to the goddess, to adults who want to reconnect with the passionate girl they once were.

The stories in this book represent some of the many visions of the Wild Girl found throughout the world. Each story is followed by commentary and activities such as building an altar, creating healing rituals, and working with dreams. You will also learn how to start your own Wild Girls' Circle.

The twelve Wild Girl myths include:
- Luonnotar (Finland): Daughter of Nature, World Creator
- Gestinanna (Sumeria): Dreamteller in the Land of Death
- Sedna (Arctic North): The Girl Who Would Not Marry
- Artemis (Greece): Midwife to Herself
- Finola (Ireland): White Shoulder, White Wings
- Kuan Yin (China): Until Every Living Thing Is Holy

1-56718-442-1, 240 pp., 7½ x 9⅛, illus. $14.95

Silver RavenWolf

Halloween: Customs, Recipes & Spells

Grab your flowing cape and journey through the history and magickal practices of America's favorite scary holiday. From Old World roots to New World charm, you will traverse the hodgepodge of legends and customs that created our modern tradition. *Halloween* brings you serious facts based on accurate research, as well as practical, how-to goodies and gossipy tidbits. Learn how history created many inaccurate myths about the original Halloween, which the ancient Celts called "Samhain," and how modern pagans still view it as a religious celebration. Discover practices, rituals, and recipes that honor the spirit of the holiday, which you can adapt to fit any spiritual orientation.

1-56718-719-6, 264 pp., 7½ x 9⅛, illus. $12.95

Dorothy Morrison

Yule:
A Celebration of
Light and Warmth

The "holidays": some call them Christmas or Hanukkah, others know them as Los Posadas or Ta Dhiu. Still others celebrate Winter Solstice or Yule. They are a time for reflection, resolution, and renewal. Whatever our beliefs, the holidays provide us with rituals to celebrate the balance of light and dark, and for welcoming the healing powers of warmth back into our world.

Jam packed with more than sixty spells, invocations, and rituals, *Yule* guides you through the magic of the season. Traveling its realm will bring back the joy you felt as a child—the spirit of warmth and good will that lit the long winter nights. Discover the origin of the eight tiny reindeer, brew up some Yuletide coffee, and learn ways to create your own holiday traditions and crafts based on celebrations from a variety of countries and beliefs.

1-56718-496-0, 216 pp., 7½ x 9⅛, 56 illus. $17.95